A QUESTION OF COURAGE

Em could hardly credit her own daring – here she was, Emily Palmer from the back streets of Birmingham, carrying a placard that boldly read VOTES FOR WOMEN in a bicycle parade, and on a Sunday, too! Her Dad would have clouted her and her Mam died of shame if they'd known. But Em had been swept into the cause by the eloquent Louise Marshall, and though their lives were worlds apart, Emily knew she'd had enough of being a 'bloomin' slave'. Already she'd spent five years sewing for a pittance and she was only eighteen.

The night that Emily and Louise were caught red-handed painting slogans on the golf course sealed their friendship and their fight. Next came London and Mrs Pankhurst's Suffragette Movement and the cloak and dagger fun was over. Now it was rallies, window-smashing, convictions, imprisonments, and most terrible of all – force feeding. But as the movement and its violence grew, so did Emily's self-doubts, and for her the choice of continuing the fight became a question of courage.

MARJORIE DARKE

A
QUESTION
OF COURAGE

Illustrated by Janet Archer

FONTANA LIONS

First published 1975 by Kestrel Books
First published in Fontana Lions 1978
by William Collins Sons & Co. Ltd
8 Grafton Street, London W1X 3LA
Fourth impression July 1985

© 1975 by Marjorie Darke

Printed and bound in Great Britain by
William Collins Sons & Co. Ltd, Glasgow

For Lance Salway

1

THERE *must* be an end to this day! Minutes stretching like elastic, making weeks out of every second. It wouldn't be so bad if there was a clock, but there was nothing to go by except the low sunlight thinning through Birmingham smoke, which spread warm patches across her back and on to the workroom floor. Another week or two and they would be working by gaslight. Never mind that! It was today that mattered, this wonderful day, so achingly long ...

The doorbell tinkled distantly from down the stairs, smothered by the rhythmical whirr of the treadle sewing machine. One of the girls stitching giggled over a whispered remark. The bell sounded with greater insistence. Mrs Harris, red-faced and perspiring, emerged from the privacy of the fitting-room, a pincushion on her wrist like a small hedgehog.

'Go and see who that is, Emily. I'm only halfway round

Mrs Craig's hem. Don't know who it can be at this time of day, I'm sure. There's no more fittings and only half an hour before we close.'

Emily stopped sewing. Not long and yet a lifetime. To have to sit here pushing a needle in and out, waiting . . . waiting, with all that longing inside . . .

'Emmie, wake up! Ma 'Arris is talking to yo!' A nudge and a whisper from fat Ada sitting alongside.

'What's that?' Emily came to with a start.

'Emily Palmer, stir yourself! I don't pay you to day-dream. Get down the stairs and see who's at the door. If it's a customer, show her into the parlour.' There was a shrill edge to Mrs Harris's voice, a sure sign that the fitting was proving tiresome.

Snatched from her thoughts, Emily put down the night-gown she was tucking and hastily retreated to the dark passage, clattering down steep stairs to a narrow box of a hall where an unlit gas-mantle jutted dangerously. She ducked from experience and opened the door.

'Good afternoon! Mrs Harris is expecting me. Tell her Miss Marshall is here . . . Miss *Louise* Marshall.'

The young woman on the doorstep was as small as herself, but there comparison ended. The broad cheek-bones and stocky body, which Emily carried around with resignation, took on an abrasive coarseness beside this fine-boned elegance topped by the most fashionable hat of tulle and pheasant feathers, from beneath which an abundance of rich bronze hair struggled to be free. A pair of wide-set greenish eyes regarded her with authority. There was authority in the voice too; the kind that comes with money. And money there obviously was. Parked close to the kerb was the biggest, most sumptuous motor car Emily had ever seen. Polished to high perfection, it dazzled the eye with the sun glinting off two sets of brass carriage lamps and the brass hinges and bindings of the long cylindrical bonnet. Acres of maroon bodywork stand-ing in tall stateliness on huge spider wheels gleamed like Ernie's Sunday boots.

'Well, aren't you going to tell your mistress I'm here?'

Emily felt resentment prickle, thinking – she takes me

8

for a skivvy. She stepped aside, trying to keep her voice colourless. 'Mrs Harris said for yo to wait in the parlour.'

The girl turned, signalling to the smartly dressed man sitting at the wheel of the car. 'Wait for me, Peter. I'll not be long.'

Inside the dark overstuffed parlour she sat down on one of the high-backed tapestry chairs and prepared to wait with impatience.

Emily said: 'I'll tell Mrs Harris yo're here.' This was going to set the cat amongst the pigeons! Ma Harris would be in a right old sweat, what with Mrs Craig's pernickety ways and this one with her hoity-toity manner. Worse still, it would delay the wage-paying. And that meant . .

A cold chill brought out sweat under her armpits and down her back. Bunching up her long serge skirt, exposing sturdy legs in darned wool stockings, she took the stairs two at a time, and came face to face with the large expanse of Mrs Craig's silk-draped bosom . . . and the awful frown of her employer.

'Miss Palmer . . . REALLY!'

Old cow, Emily thought, wanting to say it out loud, but refraining. There was no point in sacrificing nine and sixpence a week, miserable though it was; especially today. She pulled her face into a semblance of a shame.

'I'm sorry, Mrs Craig,' flattening herself against the banisters. 'A young lady to see yo, Mrs Harris, Miss Louise Marshall. I took her into the parlour like yo said.'

Now they were all going to have to wait for their money. Damn Miss Louise Marshall! Why did she have to come today? Some mess over the date.

'Get back to your work then,' Mrs Harris said sharply.

'She's all of a do-dah,' fat Ada said, nodding so that her fair curls bobbed. 'Who was it?'

'Oh, I don't know . . . some stuck-up miss.' Emily sat down heavily. The fading October sun seemed too hot now through the glass and her sweating hands made the cotton squeak.

'Go on, tell us . . . tell us!' They were all agog, bored with long hours of sewing; avid for anything that hinted gossip. Five of them, all shapes and sizes, tied together

9

by two common bonds, their youth and the need to earn a living. Except Vera, bent over the treadle sewing machine, feet moving steadily. Vera never took part in any little flurries of excitement. She hid her thoughts well, looking out at the world with wary suspicion through large hazel eyes.

Emily idled, hating the tucks, hating the customer who was prolonging this never-ending Saturday, almost hating Vera because of the way she was, all secrets and scorn, with barely a decent word for Vic who was daft about her. Emily felt the almost-hatred rise a degree at the thought of this treatment of her brother.

Alice was impatient. 'Don't be so aggravating, Emmie! Who was it?'

'Said her name was Miss Marshall . . . Miss *Louise* Marshall.' Emily gave a fair imitation of the imperious voice.

'Yo're a turn, Emmie!' Flo giggled as she always did. If she scorched her sewing with too hot a flat iron and lost some of her wages, she would still giggle.

'Miss *Louise* Marshall!' Emily repeated, egged on to further exaggeration.

Vera looked round sharply. Emily was quick to notice her reaction and saw a flicker of recognition in the pinched white face. 'Someone yo knows?' she called, but Vera turned back to her work again and didn't answer.

Down below a door banged, footsteps came to the bottom of the stairs and Mrs Harris called up:

'Bring that bolt of green silk down here, Emily, and look sharp about it.'

'In favour today, Emmie,' Alice said.

'Favour? Bloomin' slave yo means.' Emily flung down the nightgown and stamped across to the fitting-room where several rolls of material were stacked on a long table. Selecting one, she pulled it roughly towards her, catching the end between the table and its flap. There was a sharp ripping sound.

'Bloody thing!' Emily said with loud venom.

'Spit it into the wind, duck, while yo're out of earshot,'

Alice advised as Emily stalked back through the work-room.

'That's not the half of what I'm thinking,' Emily said darkly.

It was past seven-thirty before the door closed behind Miss Louise Marshall, and a ruffled Mrs Harris summoned her staff into the sanctuary of the fitting-room to collect their wages.

With the money clutched in her hand, Emily flung on her coat jabbing pins through felt hat and untidy hair, not waiting to gather up the wisps, running down the stairs into the street. The 'What's got into 'er' and 'Where's the fire' floated over her head, unanswered. She ran flat out the whole length of Albion Street, crossed the cobbles past the corner shop, turned sharp left along the sleazy confines of Cockpit Alley and left again into a long grey street where narrow rows of grimy terraced houses leaned on the pavement. There was little gaslight here. The sun had gone and twilight was pulling in the shadows. Emily ran on, nose dripping, one stocking wrinkling below a loose garter. Halfway down the street she turned into an entry leading to a square court surrounded by mean houses. A cat perched on the lichen-covered slates of the communal wash-house, unperturbed by a group of ragged children dodging round the walls in a fast game of tig, their bare feet slapping on the blue-brick paving. Emily tried to quieten her breathing, keeping out of sight in the shadows. A few lights glimmered, but the windows of the house at which she stared anxiously, were dark. There was not even the dim flicker of a candle.

'Yo looking for Mrs Nailor, duck?'

Startled, Emily turned to see next-door's Gran peering from her doorway.

'Down the pub drinking this week's 'ousekeeping and the week after.' The old woman cackled. 'Yo the girl that's been coming these past ten Saturdays? Paying 'er something 'ave yo? She's off down the shop like greased lightning soon as yo've turned the corner. No borrowing a screw of tea then. It's 'alf a pound *and* a lardy cake as like as not.'

'I'll try the pub,' Emily said, wanting to stem the old woman's babble.

'I'll tell 'er yo've been here. What name is it?'

'It don't matter,' Emily muttered, backing away and hurrying down the entry. She wanted desperately to peer into the kitchen, just for a glimpse, to make sure it was safe, but dared not with those inquisitive eyes watching. In the street she paused a moment, knowing it was playing with fire not going straight home. Mam would be waiting, ready with the edge of her tongue and a dollop of slaps. She took a long hard breath to still the butterflies. What did a hiding matter? Hadn't she felt plenty of those and lived? Nothing mattered except paying the last shilling and sixpence. Then it would be hers, all hers for ever and ever.

The journey to the pub seemed endless even though she took the short cut past the Church school. Iron railings caged the empty yard, strangely forlorn without the shouts of playing children. She never passed without a tug of regret for those far off school-days. Five years since she left, and sewing ever since with the prospect of going on at Ma Harris's for another five and beyond. The thought was enough to make you sick. It was like being bundled into a parcel, tied to dressmaking and no likelihood of anything more interesting turning up. Sometimes she felt such a red-hot longing to be free that it was a wonder her clothes didn't scorch. Not that there was the least point in getting in a tizzy about her 'station' as Mam was fond of saying. What could a working girl expect; any girl for that matter? It was only the rich ones that could live as they pleased. Once she had thought of being a school-teacher, like Miss Barnes, wearing a white blouse with a high starched collar and tie. Hair in a bun and little specs balanced on the end of her nose; severe yet kind and always, *always* just. Emily sighed and tore the dream into shreds once and for all. When you left school at twelve and there were no books to be had and no time for reading anyway, it was a waste longing for things that could never be. Besides, she had other fish to fry.

Across the street the lights from the 'George and

Dragon' shone with welcome. Someone was playing 'Daisy, Daisy, give me your answer do' on the tinny piano. Emily felt excitement and apprehension screwing up inside in case her Dad was already there. He'd want to know what she was at and nobody had to know. Not yet! Not until she was ready. A wind blew along the street catching at bits of litter, spinning them into a whirligig dance as she pushed open the door into the pub. The air met her thick and strong with stale smells of beer, smoke, old clothes and trodden sawdust. Red Sam was serving behind the bar.

'Your Dad not coming tonight, Emmie?' Sweat was rolling off him, down his nose, dripping into the tankard he held.

Emily shrugged. 'I was looking for Mrs Nailor.' No sign of her Dad then. He must still be at home in the tub scrubbing off the week's coal-dust.

'Mrs Nailor is it . . . thought your Mam had sent yo for a pint to take home. Someone said she'd been on the rampage 'cause yo were late from work.' Red Sam was looking round the bar as he talked, but there was no need.

'Just come at the right moment, lovie.' Mrs Nailor got up from a table by the little round window with the picture of St George fighting the dragon, and clutched her arm. 'Gimme that one and a tanner . . . another gin, Sam, and none of yo skimping.'

Sam rolled his eyes, looking towards the ceiling for Emily's benefit as he poured the drink.

'Please, Mrs Nailor, can't we go back now?' Emily pleaded.

'What's the rush?' Mrs Nailor was sipping her gin, licking thin lips with relish.

'I've got to get back home or Mam'll skin me. Please, Mrs Nailor!'

'Oh all right then!' She downed the gin, coughed and wiped water from her reddened eyes.

Emily was afraid she might be tipsy, but if she was, it hardly showed, though the walk back to her house took so long Emily felt she would scream. Mrs Nailor shuffled up the entry, fumbling in her pocket for her key. It took her some moments to find the keyhole. The lock appeared to be stiff and she grunted. At last the door into the kitchen was open. Emily strained to see, but could make out nothing in the darkness. Suppose it wasn't there . . . suppose it had been pinched . . . suppose . . . She held her breath, almost hearing the seconds creak by on leaden feet as Mrs Nailor poked about finding oil lamp and matches. As the shadows receded Emily stood very still. There was the bicycle, *her* bicycle, outlined against the whitewashed wall in soft lamplight. The reality of it gave her a shock, even though she had every detail imprinted on her memory. Black and upright, the curved bar of the frame, handlebars that gleamed like silver. Under a metal guard the chain was partially hidden and fine strings radiated over the rear wheel as protection against wind-blown skirts. The gentle light concealed the traces of rust and scratch-marked paintwork she knew were there. It looked brand new. And it was hers . . . for ever.

'Take it, duck. Yo deserve it.' There was grudging admiration in Mrs Nailor's voice.

In a dream Emily manoeuvred the bicycle out of the kitchen, down the entry and into the street. The leather saddle was smooth under her hand and the coldness of the handlebars sent shivers up her arm. A cart rattled over the cobbles, but she neither saw nor heard. Dare she ride home? She knew she could ride in a wobbly way, having practised on Vic's bike, careering up and down the back entry when Mam was out, swerving round terrified cats and colliding with the walls. She still had the bruises to show for it. Perhaps it would be quicker and safer to walk. Wisdom won and she set off briskly on foot, feeling strangely secure in the magic of ownership so that even the sight of May's anxious face as she waited at the bottom of their entry brought no qualms, only a rapid plan of action.

'Emmie, where yo been? Mam's flaming mad.' May caught sight of the bicycle and gawped.

'Get back to the house, May, and keep Mam busy a minute,' Emily whispered. And when her sister failed to move: 'Get a move on, can't yo?' Immediately she was sorry, seeing May stumble in her anxiety to do as she was asked, painfully limping towards the yard on thin black-stockinged legs supported by irons. Emily waited. The back door slammed. Now for it! She'd better look slippy. Ghost quiet, she sneaked up the entry, peering through the darkness until she could make out the pile of old sacks Vic used to cover his bike. There were more than enough and she hid her bicycle beneath them, taking care not to scrape metal on metal. Then going back into the entry, walked noisily towards the back door, opened it and called:

'Sorry I'm late, Mam. We had this customer come unexpected.'

2

EMILY yawned and paused to look out of the kitchen window into a grey sunless morning. Yesterday's wind had blown in the rain, leaving the yard pitted with puddles and the window-panes streaked with dirt. She yawned again. Waiting filled her with yawns.

'Yo'll turn inside out one of these days,' Mam said, twitching bacon over in the frying-pan so that it sizzled and spat up a shower of fat – the Sunday treat. She was in a remarkably good temper having got rid of her spleen the night before. But even that might have been worse. Emily had handed over the remains of her wages and escaped with a cuff, helped by Dad shouting wasn't anyone going to wash his bloody back or was he going to sit there till he turned into a bloody prune?

'I'm starved!' Ernie came into the kitchen in his stockinged feet, holding his boots, braces black against the white of his Sunday shirt. 'Where's my stiff collar, Mam?'

The temperature in the kitchen dropped several degrees. Emily sensed Mam marshalling her forces of God and the Devil, but all she said was:

'Emmie, get it out the drawer.'

'Why can't he get it himself?'

'Do as you're told, girl!' The warning note sounded clear.

Emily went out into the passage, glowering at her eldest brother as she passed, his smug expression adding fuel to her resentment. She'd been up since six, lighting the range, fetching water from the pump, boiling the kettle, washing up last night's pots, then fetching and boiling more water to make tea. After that she'd set the breakfast table and peeled potatoes for dinner, not to mention polishing Dad's boots and Mam's and her own, ready for Morning Service. She'd have May to do as well, not that she minded. She'd do anything for May. But it got her goat having to run round three brawny grown men. 'A woman's place', Mam said. There was an answer to that, one she daren't say aloud – too many bad words.

The collar was rigid and polished to a high sheen with soap and a hot iron. She ran a finger over the surface. There was something satisfying about a thing well done, even if it was Ernie's and had taken her ten minutes of arm-aching work to achieve.

'Shan't be wanting that thing,' Dad said, coming out of the bedroom and mistaking the collar for his. He had a 'morning after' look that came from too little booze rather than too much. Emily wasn't sure which was worse. His short stubbly hair stood straight up and his eyes were squeezed with sleep. 'Tell yo Mam I'm not coming to church.' He went down the stairs and out to the privy in the yard.

Leaving her to do the dirty work again! Why couldn't he tell Mam himself? But she knew the answer – he was as nervous of stirring things as she was. This day was in danger of becoming twice as frustrating as yesterday. A row was on the boil. She had seen the signs. It was the same every Sunday since Ernie had taken to going to Chapel instead of Church. Dad's threat to stay at home would be the final straw. Well, let them wait, both of them!

May was sitting on the bed when Emily went into their bedroom, one stocking on, the other fallen out of reach beneath the rush-bottomed chair. She looked up, eyes huge and dark in her pointed white face.

'Is it all right, Emmie, have yo looked?'

They had talked in whispers for hours last night, in the big brass bed they shared. May knew every detail of the bicycle, could see the curve of the frame, feel the smoothness of the brown leather saddle, smell the oil on the chain and hear the creak of the springs.

'How should I know?' Emily said with a trace of bitterness as she picked up the stocking and rolled it ready to put on. 'I've not had a chance to look.' She relented, seeing familiar anxiety creep into May's expression. 'But it's sure to be safe, dry enough too. Vic's sacks will have

17

kept out the rain.'

'Will you try it soon?'

There was no trace of envy in her question and Emily felt a swell of compassion that was choking.

'Not yet. Put your foot in here.' It was pitifully thin. On with the irons, cumbersome things with thick leather straps at thigh, knee and ankle. 'Tell yo what . . . first chance we get I'll give yo a ride. I'll hold yo safe and yo're small enough for your legs not to get in the way of the pedals.'

'Oo, Emmie, will yo?' Delight shining in the big eyes, bringing tears.

'Yo first, then me.' It was the biggest sacrifice Emily could think of before Mam's voice rang out, shattering their secret conversation. Emily scuttled out, picking up the collar from the chest of drawers at the top of the stairs. Vic was before her and turned to pull her mouse hair which she hadn't yet brushed. He caught her waist, spun her round and kissed both cheeks boisterously. She couldn't help laughing and some of the cobwebs of irritation fell away: a hand through his wiry hair making it stand like a cock's-comb before going down and sedately placing Ernie's collar on the table beside his wodge of bread. Ernie grunted, but took no further notice. He was studying some pamphlet to do with the Wrath of God. Much good may it do yo, Emily thought, hoping shrewishly that he would splash bacon fat on the collar. Then immediately feeling guilt because she loved Vic and disliked Ernie. The Bible said she ought to love everyone as much as herself and try though she might, it was impossible. Even within her own family it was impossible. There were so many feelings washing about inside her, tossing her helplessly like a cork in the sea. Was everybody the same? It was difficult to know when you weren't inside their skin.

'Dad isn't coming to church,' she said, to punish herself.

'Oh he isn't, isn't he? We'll see about that. The very idea! As if it weren't bad enough my eldest son following the Devil's beckoning finger, preaching Satan's words on street corners . . . dishonouring God's holy teaching . . .

spitting on the sacred places of the Lord with your heathen ways. Oh yo can shrug your shoulders, my lad, but when Judgement Day comes it won't be your name that the Angels call. And when Gabriel blows his trumpet and the Holy Ones are singing God's praises yo'll be down below stoking up them fires . . . see if yo likes that! Yo'll likely want to change your ways when yo're racked with pain that burns hotter than one of them furnaces at your brass foundry. I've spent my life trying to push yo into the Way of Righteousness, but yo're as pig-headed as most men and more so than some. Set on the downward path and there's no turning yo . . .'

In spite of herself Emily was fascinated. She didn't agree with one word, but there was no denying when Mam got under way the words flowed out smooth as silk and just as strong. It must be good to say things as you wanted, the words coming easy, not struggling or going dry like she did when powerful feelings were on her.

Dad came in buttoning his trousers and the flow became a torrent, until he cut across with: 'Stop that bloody nagging! It's getting so a man can't be master in his own house.'

Mam slapped bacon and fried bread on a plate, shoving it on the table before him. 'If yo was to act proper there'd be no need for me to speak up. Ernie learns his heathen ways from yo. Given a strong example by his Dad he'd never have swerved from the Church.' She glared at Ernie, who pushed more food in his mouth, chewing in obstinate silence. 'Playing dumb now are yo . . . both of yo . . .' as Dad said nothing either. 'There's nothing to choose between the pair of yo. Where's your dignity and principles?'

Her final remark seemed to touch a sensitive spot. Banging both fists on the table, Dad roared: 'Shut up, woman! Yo gets worse every day. Woman isn't to fling her weight about. Bad as them Suffragettes gabbing all the time about principles and such stuff. Go and join 'em if yo likes. Throw a few bombs, burn a few houses and smash a few windows. It'll maybe get rid of your bad temper and give us some peace.'

'Don't yo dare class me with them hussies,' Mam shouted. 'I'm a God-fearing woman and don't yo forget it. I wouldn't have anything to do with that lot if my life depended on it.'

Emily shrivelled inside, waiting for the pots to start flying, but something damped Dad's anger. He returned to his food mumbling: 'Gab on if yo likes, I'm not agoing.'

But he did. They all did, except Ernie who went off to Chapel followed by a cloud of Mam's disapproval. Emily sat through the service and Mr Boddington's interminable sermon feeling as if she was sinking into a sticky bowl of mutton fat. The words congealed round her, glueing her down so she would never free herself. And all the time she was experiencing her bicycle, the wind in her face, pedalling faster and faster . . .

A sharp dig in the ribs and Mam's whispered command: 'Kneel!'

Muzzy with dreams, Emily heard the Blessing. The organ blared out and Mr Boddington moved in stately fashion towards the vestry. There were hours and hours to wait yet, Emily knew. If God was listening he couldn't miss her prayers for the chance of a real ride this afternoon. Please let Dad have a lie-down on the bed and Mam get stuck in her Bible reading in the parlour like most Sundays. Ernie would be off preaching and Vic and May were on her side. The prayers clamoured in her head, but uneasy doubts clung round. Things didn't often work out as you wished.

Sunday stew with the melting dumplings she usually loved, stuck in her throat today. May was staring across the table, pink blotches on her cheeks. Excited.

'Yo aren't sickening for something, May?' Mam put a hand on her forehead.

Emily sweated. Someone would guess. She'd never get away with it. Riding on a Sunday . . . any day . . .

'Pass us the salt, Ernie. Applie pie for afters, Mam? There's no one makes pastry like yo.' Vic gave Emily a wink. The moment passed. But there was clearing the table, dishes to do. Women's work. Emily mashed the tea. Took a cup to Mam in the parlour and another upstairs to Dad in the darkened bedroom. Perhaps God had been listening after all.

May was waiting in the kitchen. She pulled herself up when Emily came in. 'Can we go now? Is it safe?'

'I think so.' Emily went into the yard, through the back gate and out to the entry. It was empty except for a dog sniffing along the walls. She scanned the neighbouring yards and houses for prying eyes. No one but old Mr Green pottering round his tubs of straggly chrysanthemums. Sunday quiet. It wouldn't last, but they were safe for the moment. She went back into the yard, lifted the sacks and picked up the bicycle, heart hammering. 'Come on then!'

It was much more difficult getting May safely perched on the saddle than she had anticipated. Twice up and down the entry, feeling the unsteady awkward weight, guiding the handlebars with May hanging on so rigid, smiling and smiling as if about to shriek fearful delight.

'My turn now.' Emily lifted her down. Leaving her at the gate, she wheeled the bicycle down the entry into the street. There were some children skipping at the far end and two women gossiping at their front doors, but she no longer cared who saw. One thing was in her mind – this was to be the very first ride on her own bicycle. Astride the frame she settled her skirt, then hotched on to the saddle, pushing on the pedals. The effort to balance was enormous and she wobbled across the street, missing the kerb by inches, then back again. Several times she almost fell off and had to put one foot on the ground to steady herself. But she *wouldn't* give up . . . she'd rather die first. Gradually her confidence rose as she ventured along the street, so intent on staying upright she didn't see the boy coming round the corner.

'Hey . . . it's Emmie Palmer on a bike!'

Emily swerved and almost fell. Willie Green in a cut-down knickerbocker suit was trotting after her, whistling and laughing.

'Bony Emmie . . . bony Emmie, where's yo bloomers

21

gone?' he chanted in a sing-song voice.

He had passed her now, walking backwards, grinning like a loony.

Furious, Emily shoved two fingers in the air and felt a mean satisfaction when he tripped, mouth open and sat down with a bang on the pavement. Serve him right! She'd done all that, even taken one hand off the handlebars and was still balancing. She sailed round the corner past the pub, feeling tall. More people were about. Some of them knew her. The word would go round. No keeping a secret now. But who cared! Whatever the outcome she had done it; no one could take that away. A few catcalls followed her as she pedalled steadily along the street, gathering speed as the ground sloped downhill. It was a marvellous feeling skimming through the air. Easy! Birds must feel like this. Oh, it was wonderful . . . wonderful! Worth all the scrimping. Lunches of bread and lard. Doing without, if Mam was short, because she wouldn't spare even a ha'penny for the treat of a fresh cob or a bag of chitterlings. Faster and faster! The bicycle whirred; feet flying; created wind shaping the thick folds of her skirt round legs and thighs. Summer Hill Terrace came to meet her and the nerves of her stomach tightened. It was steep, very steep: parallel with Sandpits where the trams ran, a sharp bend at the bottom. But it was Sunday and traffic was sparse. A pony and trap on the far side of the road trotting briskly, one or two groups of people walking, a motor car rumbling miles up the road. It was safe enough.

Braking was not as easy. The bicycle seemed to buck like a wilful horse. Emily wrenched the handlebars to the right in order to keep her balance then back again, shooting into the wide main road out of control as the front wheel was trapped in a tram line. Behind, a car horn blared, brakes squealed, someone bellowed:

'LOOK OUT . . .'

Horror-stricken, Emily fought with the handlebars, but even without the oncoming car she knew she must fall. There was a jarring blow. The bicycle seemed to squeal for mercy and she catapulted on to the granite-hard road that jolted out every ounce of breath and telescoped her

22

bones. She lay, eyes closed, writhing, oblivious of everything except sickening pain. From the world outside her body came indistinct sounds of voices. Someone had a hand under her shoulders, lifting.

'. . . no, leave her . . . are you all right . . . couldn't avoid you . . .'

Words jumbled. Gradually the pain lessened. Oh God, the bicycle! She opened her eyes, struggling to sit up.

'Please . . . are you all right?' The girl bending over her was somehow familiar, a young man standing behind, also – Ma Harris's doorstep!

'Miss Louise Marshall,' Emily said, and then: 'My bicycle, is it . . . ?'

The girl showed no surprise at being recognized. 'No bones broken I hope. We simply couldn't help hitting you. One moment nothing, the next there you were straight in our path and not a chance of cutting round you. I'm terribly sorry.'

'My bicycle?'

'Her heart's in the right place, Lou, concerned more for her machine than her bruises.' The man picked up the bicycle. 'Bit twisted . . . nothing that can't be put right.'

'Things before people again, Peter!' Louise Marshall said tartly. 'For goodness sake give me a hand, can't you?'

'Keep calm, Lou . . . one thing at a time.'

'How do you expect me to stay calm when we are going to be late? We've cut it pretty fine as it is.' She had a hand under Emily's arm, her eyes on a neat gold wrist watch.

Emily was on her feet now, shaken and bruised, but unbroken. The fact that she seemed relatively unhurt brought a subtle change in Louise's sympathies. One or two bystanders were pressing round, anxious to share in the accident. One of them said: 'There'll be a bobby 'ere soon. Got noses fer trouble, bobbies.'

'Oh Lord . . . do something, Pete, or we'll be here for ever.'

'Righty-ho . . . who's being callous now!'

Emily watched her precious bicycle being tied to the

23

large luggage rack on the roof of the dignified car she had last seen outside Ma Harris's.

'Now you . . . upsadaisy!'

Too dazed to rebel, Emily was pushed into the back seat, the door slammed and she found herself cocooned in soft green corduroy; the driver and his passenger cut off by a glass panel. Louise turned, tapping on the window.

'Sorry and all that. I'm sure you don't mind doing a round trip, but I simply can't be late for the meeting. He'll fix your bicycle too. He's a splendid mechanic. Tinkers all the time with cars and things. Come to think of it you might like to . . .'

At this point the car came to life with a deep-throated rumble of sound. Peter let go of the starting handle and grinned over the top of the bonnet, lifting his cap and giving it a twirl.

'Oh do stop larking!' Louise shouted.

'Steady, old girl, you want to save your energies for the speechifying.' Peter climbed into the driver's seat, released the brake and revved the engine to engage the gear. With a jerk they rolled forward. A cold shower of reality sprayed over Emily bringing her back to earth for the first time since she began her bicycle ride. In panic she leaned forward, rapping the glass.

'Where are we going?'

'What?'

Loudly: 'Where are we going?'

But Louise's attention was divided and the car seemed to bound forward thrusting Emily back against the large padded seat.

A minute ago, or was it last year, she had been glorying in her newly acquired treasure, bubbling over with happiness. Now the thought of the twisted handlebars, the punctured tyre and every scratch on the paintwork hurt far more than the bruises. And it all their fault . . . no it wasn't, that was unfair. Wretched tram-lines, greasy with last night's rain, and her own lack of skill. But those two were pushing her about like an old kitchen table. She glared indignantly at the backs of their necks. Hot tears would keep coming, but she fought against crying, determined not to let them see this weakness on top of everything else. What to do? Find out where they were going . . . she had to know.

As if by telepathy Louise turned to look at the captive '. . . meeting.' Her voice was muffled by the glass panel, and in her turmoil Emily did not catch the first word. Louise saw her blank stare. 'Women's Suffrage,' she said, raising her voice as if Emily were a foreigner. 'You know – Votes for us Women!'

3

'I NEVER thought to see you here,' Vera said, her faint West Country accent made more noticeable by her amazement. 'Never in this wide world.'

'Yo're not the only one to get a surprise.' Emily was smoothing her skirt, trying to hide the tear down one side, scraping some sort of order into her flyaway hair. If only she could stop shaking!

The heavy carved furniture of the Vicarage drawing-room had been pressed back against the walls. Potted plants and knick-knacks, usually standing on occasional tables, packed the top of the rosewood piano, quite over-shadowing a pair of red candles in curling brass sconces on the front. A collection of women, most of them starched and polished to such a degree they were forced to keep themselves poker straight, filled the chairs stretching in rows across the room. Scattered among them were other shabbier women with shawls over their heads, staring round as if unsure why they had come. From one wall three sepia photographs of past vicars stared sternly down with a disapproval Emily was sure they would have felt. Mrs Boddington, the present vicar's wife, was flapping about at the far end of the room on a small raised dais crowded with two chairs and an even more crowded table: blue velvet cloth, vase of pampas-grass, carafe of water, pile of leaflets, ornate brass cross on a stand.

Emily watched Louise Marshall thread between a few people framed in the looped crimson curtains of the french window. She stepped on to the dais looking remarkably self-assured. Her movements were steady and precise, her dark green dress with ruffles of lace at neck and wrists setting off her tawny hair. The word 'Perfect' came into Emily's mind. There was an indefinable quality about her that compelled attention. A great contrast to Mrs Boddington's ineffectual flustered twitching. Emily

26

had a fleeting vision of Mr Boddington proclaiming 'Votes for Women' from the pulpit. The church roof would fall in! And yet here was Mrs B going to let a Suffragette speak in her drawing-room!

'How did you come to hear of the meeting?' Vera asked.

'By accident,' Emily said with a wry smile. 'I came with her.'

'Who?'

'Louise Marshall.'

Vera looked at her with renewed respect and some astonishment. 'But you never let on you knew her at work?'

'I didn't then,' Emily said patiently. 'She knocked me off my . . . knocked me down, or at least this fellow who was driving the car did; on the way here.'

'That's her brother,' looking to see if Emily was cut about. 'Brings her to all the Women's Suffrage meetings, collects her too.'

'I thought they was called Suffragettes.'

'No, they're different.'

'What's the difference?'

Vera looked at her with a touch of scorn. 'Don't you never read nothing? I'd have thought you'd take an interest.'

Emily was stung. 'Oh don't be so sniffy!'

A touch of colour came into Vera's pale cheeks, but she answered mildly enough: 'We make our protest without violence. Suffragettes smash windows and burn houses, things like that.'

Emily was going to ask more questions, but Mrs Boddington clapped her hands for attention.

'Ladies . . . quiet please . . . would you be seated. I think there are enough chairs.'

The hum of conversation dwindled as latecomers, including Mr Boddington and another parson, found seats.

Mam would have a fit if she knew. Mr Boddington, a secret supporter of these 'Hussies!' But they didn't look like hussies. Stodgily respectable was a better description. Of the lot of them, she was the one who looked a sight.

There was mud all over her skirt and she still felt weepy with shock. Daft not to go home, but a kind of intense curiosity had made her stay. She *could* have let Louise's brother drive her home. What a stir that would have made in their street . . . she'd have been the talk of the neighbourhood for weeks! Instead she'd be given a slice of jaw-pie when she did get back. Don't think of it. She was here, wasn't she? Learning. You had to grab at chances or they slipped past for ever.

Mrs Boddington prepared to speak, dabbing discreetly at perspiration on her top lip with a lace-trimmed handkerchief.

'Now, ladies, I think we can resume. As you know, this meeting is a new venture for the working women in this area of Birmingham. The National Union of Women's Social Suffrage, which many of you know and cherish as a cause dear to the hearts of forward-looking ladies, has been instrumental in . . . er . . . suggesting that we try to widen our horizons. Our speaker, Miss Marshall, was one of the first to . . . er . . . be of the opinion that . . . er . . . our less fortunate . . . er . . . sisters, who after all have as much right to the Vote as . . . er . . .'

Oh get on with it! Mewing like a cat in labour! What was she saying now? Getting in knots over the less fortunate sisters. Yo, Emily Palmer . . . though Mrs B's way of puuting it is sandpaper on a graze. Come on Louise Marshall, get on your feet and let's hear if you're as snotty as I'm expecting.

Emily slid a sidelong glance at Vera, wondering why she came to meetings like this. The meek face with the tight curtains of dark hair expressed nothing she could interpret.

At last!

'Thank you, Mrs Boddington . . . ladies . . .' Louise acknowledged the clapping. 'It heartens me to see how many care for our Cause – heartens me even more to see new faces. I particularly appreciate the effort *you* have made in coming here. There are dozens of conflicting ties and duties for women and so few spare moments. This encouragement you bring, warms and strengthens. Thank

28

you for being here.'

The round tones of her voice carried easily and the warmth of her smile broke through Emily's suspicions.

'We are all here because of our concern about the position we are forced to accept in daily life, a lowly position, a degrading position. It is the result of continuous injustice from an endless past, the product of a mindless tyranny.' She paused, smiling again. 'But I'm not going to launch into a dry lecture about history and politics. This is to be an appeal to you all to join with us in the fight for decency, for justice, for the Vote – in short, for the true dignity of Woman. We must make it plain to all that our rights as human beings demand more than the scraps from Master's table! It is 1912, my friends, yet for half the population of England we might still be in the Middle Ages. Rich and poor, we are chained together and branded as "Women" . . . inferior creatures who have neither the mental powers, nor enough sense of responsibility to share in saying how our lives shall be lived. And who brands us so? Men! We are outcasts, my friends; cast out by whom? Men! They treat us as a lower order than the criminals and drunkards who are allowed to vote. This is what we must believe if the same Vote is denied to us!'

She leaned forward, supporting herself on the table, her colour heightened, her eyes searching the faces of the listening women. For a few seconds the wake of her passionate statement held them silent, then as she drew herself up and said in a more normal voice: 'We are here to discuss how this state of affairs may be changed,' a sigh came from the audience, and then silence again.

'There are women all over England banding together, using a variety of titles, to campaign against this injustice. The National Union of Women's Social Suffrage which sponsored this meeting and to which many of you already belong. Then there is the Women's Freedom League . . . Birmingham's own Miss Kirby's Franchise Club . . . the Women's Social and Political Union, perhaps better known as the Suffragettes. Ah, I see you have heard of *them* . . .' as a murmur rose. 'But it isn't the name that matters, it is the principle for which we must fight, and until the majority of women realize that their one effective weapon is unity, little can be done.

'Why then isn't there one group only, you may ask? The answer is that some of us are less patient than others, and so there is disagreement about the way we should tackle this problem of ours. But never forget that the demonstrations, whatever their nature, are numerous and sincere . . . petitions; marches; chaining ourselves to railings; interrupting political meetings; refusing to pay taxes; smashing windows . . . I could go on and on. But though separate in method we have a common aim which binds us together with ropes of steel – unbreakable. Too long women have sat back subservient, meekly accepting the rules and instructions of men who know little and understand less of the needs of half the population of our country. We women may equal men in number, but do we have equivalent rights? As you scrub and cook, toil to keep bread in your family's mouths and warmth in the hearth, you know without me telling you that the answer is no . . . no . . . NO!' Banging the table with her fist, making the cross jump and leaflets slither across the cloth. 'We have no right to speak out in the running of our homes, the guardianship of our children, the government of our country. If ever injustice existed, it was never so apparent as in this.'

Stirred as she had never been before, Emily felt tears sting her eyes. Right . . . oh yes, right! A woman's place was at the kitchen sink and would remain there if things went on in the same way. Not that Miss Louise Marshall spent much time doing housework or the like – bet she never did a hand's turn – but that didn't stop her from knowing. Those three great men at home, even her lovable Vic, all expected uncomplaining service. It was her duty, Mam's, even May's! Votes for Women! She felt like shouting it up and down the streets, though a niggling voice told her that having the Vote wouldn't stop Dad from expecting his boots to be cleaned every Sunday, or get Ernie to do a bit of housework. Emily grinned at the thought of Ernie on his knees with his backside in the air, black-leading the range!

She came out of her thoughts to hear Louise saying: '. . . strength of purpose, and we must give time and effort, however small, to achieve the right to vote, the right to decide, the right to exist!'

To exist! Emily looked down at her hands with the pincushion fingers. *They* existed all right. Skin puckered and reddened with oceans of washing-up water, floor-scrubbing and fire-cleaning. Lines criss-crossing. Yes, they were real, but how could she be sure they were hers? Uncanny, looking out of your eyes at pieces of yourself. Like observing a stranger. Suddenly scared, she nipped a piece of skin between her nails and was glad to feel the sharp pinching pain.

Louise had progressed to practicalities: 'As to how you can help, I would urge you to seize every opportunity that offers itself to talk and explain, with friends, at work, in the streets if you feel prepared to speak publicly. But whatever you do, however small, nothing is too insignificant. From tiny specks of dust mountains are made, and mountains are strong and we *women* are strong.'

A spontaneous cheer came from the listeners. Emily heard herself join in. More astonishing still was the sight of Vera's animated face. Quiet, sober Vera looked like someone she'd never seen and was clapping fit to bust!

Louise held up her hand and when the enthusiasm quietened, added: 'Please don't misinterpret my reference to men. These good gentlemen here are two of a number of dedicated supporters of our right to vote. We need their support. We need every scrap of help to be had. And may I go on from there to suggest an idea I have borrowed from other members of our movement . . . a bicycle parade with placards secured to each machine. We could . . .'

'A bicycle parade?' Mrs Boddington's shocked voice interrupted. She had pushed herself to the edge of her chair, quivering.

'Yes, a bicycle parade, Mrs Boddington.' Louise's voice rang out over the buzzing whispers. 'I have three machines myself and can borrow two more. Perhaps some of you are cycling enthusiasts and would like to join the outing which I was going to suggest might take place next Sunday afternoon. As working women I know your leisure is limited, and this seems to be your only free time. Anyone who would like to know more, perhaps would see me while we have the cups of tea our hostess has so generously offered to provide. And thank you . . . thank you all.'

There was a moment's stunned silence, then more clapping, this time less enthusiastic, as if an element of doubt had crept in. Mrs Boddington rose to make a brief stammering speech of thanks and say a word about future meetings, handing out leaflets, scurrying from the dais afterwards as if her bloomers were on fire. There was a scraping of chairs; tea and biscuits were served in the gloomy dining-room. Emily pushed through the crowd, forgetting her dishevelled appearance, determined to get to Louise and discover more about the bicycle parade, even though the very thought of bicycles made her sick inside. Vera stalked after her. They found Louise, cup in hand, talking to an elderly woman in a black shawl. Waiting, Emily looked up at Vera and was struck by the comic sight they must be. Vera tall, thin, angular and buttoned down, while she looked like a square scarecrow, washerwoman's muscles and flying hairpins.

As the elderly woman moved away, Louise turned to them, beaming. 'You will come on the parade, won't you?' She looked at Emily. 'I know you have a bicycle.'

Emily felt cold and all the comedy slid away. 'Damaged,' she said.

Vera was doing the nearest thing to gaping.

'Never knew you had a bicycle!'

'Yo don't know everything.' Emily's rudeness was unfair, but she was too confused to think.

'It's all right, you know.' Louise put an arm impulsively round her shoulder, squeezing her. 'Pete's tophole with machines. You'll see when you come to our house next Sunday, for the parade. It'll be as good as new . . . better even. Say you'll come.'

Emily didn't know whether to give in and howl, or

shrivel up with the awkward feelings produced by Louise's easy show of sympathy. She stood there wishing she was anywhere but in this room. Across the dining table a grandfather clock frowned, striking four o'clock, each chime an accusation. She ought to be home. There was the tea to get, and May would be worried sick. Worse still Mam would be firing questions at her thick and fast.

'You will, won't you?' Louise was nothing if not persistent.

'All right.' Emily would agree to anything just to end the interview.

'Splendid . . . and you, Miss Bradshaw?'

Vera looked uncomfortable. 'I've got no bicycle.'

'Then you can borrow one of mine. That's settled. Three o'clock shall we say, next Sunday? We'll start from my house, in Hardwick. I haven't quite worked out the route. A round trip, I think, but it should be pleasant. We'll take a picnic; make a real afternoon's outing. It'll be great fun.' Under the influence of her smile they both forgave her bossy manner.

Mrs Boddington came weaving through the knots of women, giving away words with smiles that did not conceal her anxiety.

'Oh, Miss Marshall, about the . . . er . . . bicycle parade. Before you go any further with it, I felt I . . . er . . . must ask if you really think that . . . er . . .'

'It's all arranged, Mrs Boddington. Three o'clock next Sunday, from the Tower House. We'll be expecting you!' Louise said airily.

You could almost see the little devil sitting on her shoulder, three-pronged fork and pointed tail. She was a star turn! Fancy having the nerve to talk like that to a vicar's wife!

Demolished, Mrs Boddington gave a little gasp and sidled away. Louise was caught up in conversation with two earnest ladies in identical dark-brown velvet dresses, who obviously knew her well. Feeling like a stranger, Emily wanted to get away more urgently than ever.

'Yo coming, Vera?'

Vera shook her head, halfway through a cup of tea.

'See yo tomorrer then.'

The relief of getting away was so great, Emily forgot about saying goodbye. Closing the front door she thought suddenly, Tower House . . . where was it? Hardwick? She had a vague notion of the direction, but there was no street name. What did it matter, she probably wouldn't go.

'I say . . . wait a minute . . .'

Emily turned round. The maroon car stood at the kerb with Peter Marshall holding open one of the doors. She hesitated and he beckoned.

'Aren't you coming with us? I thought Lou said . . .'

'It's all right. I'm walking.'

'But you're limping.'

It was true. The bang on her knee was stiffening. 'It don't matter.'

He ran a hand through hair the same bronze colour as his sister's. They were alike. Faces where expressions changed easily. Wide generous mouths. But the eyes were different. His were toffee-coloured.

'I've had a quick look over your bike.' He seemed to know this would stop her from walking on. 'I've straightened the handlebars and Gardiner's mending the puncture this very minute. A dab or two of paint and you'll never know anything happened.'

'Oh, thanks!' They were alike in the way they made you feel awkward too; high-class, with those tea-and-cucumber-sandwich voices.

'She's still talking, I suppose . . . in there.' He indicated the dark-red brick and bay windows of the Vicarage.

Emily nodded.

'Right. We might as well get you home. There's plenty of time. Once she gets on her hobby-horse the clock means nothing.' He was shepherding her across the road towards the car, hand under her elbow. In spite of dismay because she was no longer in charge of herself, she felt an uplift of grandeur. What a way to arrive in their street! It would be worth all the clouts that would come once the back door was closed.

'Back seat or front, madam?'

'Front,' she said, wilting a little under so much attentive charm.

When she was installed he got into the driver's seat and adjusted various knobs and levers, then climbed down again, went to the front of the car and carefully turned the starting handle.

'What did you think of it?' he asked.

'The meeting?'

He nodded.

'It was very interesting,' she said with reserve.

'You've been bitten then.' There was a patronizing note in his voice that alerted her defences. She stared with silent suspicion which he took for lack of understanding. 'Filled with enthusiasm . . . down with those fiendish men!' He got back in the car beside her, waving a gloved hand. 'Women for ever . . .'

A wave of indignation swallowed her up. 'Miss Marshall talked a lot of sense,' she said tightly.

'She would certainly talk *a lot*!' he replied.

They were bowling along a street edging the canal. A fresh breeze, roused by the speed of the car, ruffled and tugged at Emily's hair. To be travelling with such swift grand style ought to have been exhilarating, but everything was being spoiled by his barbed jokes. Her annoyance was drying the words, but she managed to snap out:

'They was true them things she said.'

'Oh I grant you she knows how to twist words about enough to make anyone believe black's white. A born wheedler, old Lou. Had the knack from the cradle. I pull her leg about it, y'know, but it's a good thing really. Take this Women's Suffrage lark. She puts it to good use there – pulls in the crowds. And after all, where's the harm? Gives the blue-stockings something to think about!'

Emily was seething with fury. The ferocity of her reaction startled and bewildered her, so that she couldn't say anything at all. As they sailed into home ground the savour was lost. She didn't care that doors and windows were suddenly full of neighbours urgently needing to look into the street, or that May was at the entry, all the astonishment in the world netted in her expression.

Peter brought the car to a gentle halt, got out and came round to assist her. She should have felt like a queen, or a duchess at least, instead of a girl boiling with hot rage. After all it was only a joke. But his politeness just made things worse.

'I'll get Gardiner to bring your bicycle back,' Peter said. Emily made up her mind.

'Yo needn't trouble,' she told him. 'I have to come to the Tower House next Sunday afternoon for the bicycle parade. I'll collect it then.'

A variety of expressions chased each other across his face, ending with a smile that dissolved into a guffaw of laughter. 'Oh, Lou . . . a bicycle parade . . . what will you think of next! Just wait till Father hears this one!'

He was still laughing when Emily gave up trying to pass on her fury by glaring. She ran across the cobbles, pushing May aside without a word, meaning to hide in the privy until she could calm herself. But she had no chance. She was caught and held in her mother's bear-hug.

'Yo all right, girlie?'

There was no chance even to say a single word.

'Yo little devil!' Her mother held her away. 'Frightening the life out of us. We thought yo was dead.' She slapped her hard across the cheek. 'That's for all the trouble yo caused.' Another blow: 'And that's for making an indecent show of yourself, riding a *bicycle* on the Lord's Day.'

Emily tried to protect her singing head from Mam's slapping hand.

'And where yo been ever since?' Thump! 'Willie Green came with tales about yo scandalizing the street, showing your legs.' Bang! 'Then our Ernie says Joe Nailor saw yo knocked down by a motor car.'

'Oh, don't, Mam, don't!' May was plucking at her sleeve.

'I'll thump yo an' all, missie!'

As if this wasn't enough, Emily heard Dad shouting from the house:

'Wheer's the bloody little tart?'

She tried to duck the swipe he took at her as he lunged into the yard, but she was not quick enough and went reeling back against the wooden slats of the fence. He'd been at the drink, like always on a Sunday. Face suffused dark-red, mottling under his chin. There were enough bottles of booze in reserve under his bed to float a battleship! Bile rose in her throat. Hadn't she been punished enough by being knocked down and having her bicycle mangled? But there was more to come, she knew it and curled up, hands over her ears.

'Leave her alone, can't yo.'

Emily opened her eyes hardly daring to believe that Vic would come to her defence. He was there with his shirt sleeves rolled up, the strength of muscle in his forearms matching Dad's. Enough to make Dad hesitate . . a second.

'Yo keep out of it!'

'If yo gives over.'

'God damn it . . .'

She could see Vic was scared stiff, but there was something else too. He struck out, had to; a cold sickening crunch. Blood spurted and May screamed. Emily was silent.

'Go it, young 'un. Give the bugger a taste of his own medicine . . . tanner on young Vic to win.' Neighbours were crowding up the entry, overflowing into the yard, wooed from the sight of the handsome car by the promise of a good fight. Their leech-like interest cut the strings of Mam's tongue.

'Vipers,' she screeched inconsequentially. 'Long-noses! Ain't yo got nothing better to do than mind other folks' business? Get out of my sight or may the flames of Hell take yo!' She turned on her two men, raining blows left and right. 'I'll not have yo scrapping on the Lord's Day!'

Vic yelled: 'Get out of it, Emmie . . . run!'

Still dazed, Emily scrambled to her feet and fled indoors, making for the cupboard under the stairs in whose gloomy depths she had hidden all her childhood miseries. The smells of moth balls and onions were strung about with hard-pressing memories of past beatings. She crouched on the upturned orange box, trying to muffle sounds of the outside world by pulling her grandpa's cape round her.

It was a very brief respite. Minutes later the others came into the kitchen, Dad still shouting that he'd flay the skin off her.

'Hear me, girl? If I ketch yo going with a fancy man agin, I'll swing for yo . . .'

With tears rolling down her cheeks, Emily let out a short high-pitched giggle. He'd done it again! How could he always get things so wrong? She could hear him bumping about the kitchen muttering curses that rose into occasional shouts of: 'Are yo listening, m'girl?' How could she do anything else? Great brainless beer-soaked pudding!

Another giggle and another . . .

In desperation she crammed both fists against her mouth, trying to press down the mounting laughter.

4

JOSIAH MARSHALL picked up his table napkin and wiped it thoroughly across his fulsome moustache. Deliberately replacing it on the table beside his dinner plate, he went on to pick out morsels of meat from between his teeth with a silver toothpick before replying. The time lag was intentional. Louise knew it was calculated to reduce her to a quivering jelly. A trick that failed time after time. She drummed her fingers on her knee. A maid came round to collect the crockery, another followed with plum pie and cream. Louise shook her head.

'Well, may I or may I not?' she asked.

The bicycle parade hung in the balance.

Peter winked at her, gorging himself with pie.

'This time; as it is all arranged,' Josiah said grudgingly. He waved an admonishing finger. 'But listen carefully, my girl. I give you liberty beyond what most folk would, but I'll not have you making a laughing-stock of yourself or of me. I've a position to keep up.' He tapped the newspaper lying on the table. 'This Suffragette rubbish is not entering my house. Votes for Women!' He made an insult of the words, flicking at the paper again and again. 'That nonsense in there . . . that shameless hussy inciting women to go and break windows and stir up trouble in the House of Commons and anywhere else they fancy . . . the ducking-stool is what she needs. Saying it in the Albert Hall, what's more!' As if this was the final outrage.

Louise stared at him. 'If you mean Mrs Pankhurst's speech, then I'm with her all the way.'

'Fighting talk, Lou.' Peter scraped up the remains of his pie and sat back smirking. He tucked his thumbs inside his waistcoat armholes, preparing to watch the coming tussle.

'I've let you join this . . . what you call it . . . Women's Suffrage Movement. They are fools, but at least they are

39

respectable fools. A good many highly respected names. Solid financial backing.'

'You make it sound like the Stock Exchange,' Louise interrupted.

Peter blew out his cheeks, raising eyebrows. 'Sailing close to the wind!' he murmured.

Josiah and Louise turned on him at the same moment, saying:

'I'll thank you to mind your own business, sir . . .'

'Stop interfering, Peter . . .' and then immediately continued wrangling as if he weren't there.

With a shrug, Peter got up from the table and walked over to a long window, framing a garden still wet with dew. The gravelled drive wound between trim lawns linked to a shrubbery of laurel and rhododendrons. Beyond, mature lime trees spread yellowing shawls. A wind tossed their branches, releasing a shower of water and curled leaves. In spite of dappling sunlight an air of autumnal decay had settled in. Starlings came to squabble over some delicacy on the grass and flew off just as quickly, scared by two girls crunching along the gravel.

Peter broke into the arguments that were now being thrown across the table in an endless tennis match.

'Your friends, Lou. Just coming up the drive. The tall one looks worried, but that dumpy one seems bold enough.' He grinned, remembering. 'She's a firecracker. What did you say her name was?'

'Emily Palmer.'

Josiah rumbled disapproval; cheeks faintly purpling as he scented defeat. 'I don't want to see them, you hear me?' The doorbell clanged across his protest. 'Take them straight round to the stables where those infernal machines are.' He took out a gold hunter and clicked it open. 'Not even got the manners to arrive at a respectable time . . . still eating . . .'

'It *is* after half past two, Father,' Louise corrected him.

One of the maids opened the heavy mahogany door. 'Two . . . ladies to see Miss Louise.' The fractional hesitation was enough to place them firmly with the tradesmen.

Louise said with sharp emphasis: 'Well, don't leave my

friends standing in the hall. Take them into the morning-room, Jones, and bring a tray of tea.'

'And how many more of these *friends* are we to expect?' Josiah asked.

'Three. There's to be six altogether.'

'The Swashbuckling Six!' Peter flourished an imaginary sword.

With her back to her father, Louise stuck out her tongue at her brother and said to him: 'You can come at about four-thirty. You know the route, and whatever you do, don't forget the hamper.'

Josiah rapped on the table with a knife handle, commanding attention.

'A son of mine joining in these damn silly frolics. I'll not have it! Where's your sense of pride gone . . . running around after a lot of warped old maids?'

'He's only bringing the picnic, Father,' Louise said with elaborate patience. 'We can hardly balance a hamper on our handlebars.'

'Twaddle, that's what it is. Twaddle . . . d'you hear me?'

'I should think the whole house can hear. Calm down, you know it isn't good for you to get excited.' Louise was determined to remain in control.

But Josiah had no such view. He lumbered to his feet, bulky stomach pressing against the damask tablecloth. 'This is the last time, my lady. I'll not have the name of Marshall dragged through the mud. Bicycle parade!' The cultivated veneer of his voice cracked. 'Yo're right theer. Parading yoself like cattle for sale in th'markit.'

'Oh, Father . . . I'm only going for a bicycle ride and a picnic.' Louise went to him and put a hand on his arm, tweaking the end of his moustache as she had when a little girl. 'Come on, Daddy, don't be cross.'

Peter watched the familiar pattern working. Ever since their mother died it had been the same. A little wheedling, a little cosseting and Lou had won.

'A nice game of golf, that's what you need,' Louise said. She went out of the room, seconds later peeping round the door: 'Work off some of your stoutness!' disappearing, then back again: 'And your bad temper!'

You had to hand it to her. She knew just how to handle the old man! Peter smiled in admiration.

'I'll thank yo to wipe that grin off your face . . . like a cat with a bowl of cream. Where's your pride? Scrommling after a lot of daft women. It's time yo set your mind on work, my lad. Less of this shilly-shallying with motor cars and balloons. Balloons! Yo'll be building yourself a pair of wings next. Why, at your age I'd made my first thousand and got a sound business at my back *and* I was negotiating for the Foundry.'

Peter sighed, mouthing: 'Self-made man I am. Hard work and no nonsense . . .' in time with his father.

In the morning-room Emily and Vera waited in uncomfortable silence. Perched on the edge of a dark-blue velvet wing chair, Emily stared round the room. Oak panelling halfway, wallpaper of curling green leaves at the top, well-stuffed chairs, a carved oak table supporting a tiered pink and blue glass flower bowl, *and* a chiffonier. Nothing here to smooth away her discomfort or erase the blister on her heel.

'I'm that hot,' Vera said at last.

'Me too. Sweaty as an old glove,' Emily agreed. 'What I wouldn't give for a nice cup of tea.'

The door opened and Louise Marshall swept in bringing a scent of late summer laced with eau-de-cologne. Emily admired the fine cloth of her grey dress with the sailor collar, white and crisp. She felt dowdy, uncertain. The day closed in with guilty memories of May left in front of a tub of washing up. At least there hadn't been a row because nobody at home knew about the bicycle parade, except May. But the guilty feelings persisted. Pulling her elbows into her sides to hide the shiny patches on her second-hand serge suit, Emily looked up at Louise with great envy and some jealousy mixed in with her admiration. What difficulties and doubts could *she* ever have? She certainly wouldn't have had her ear chewed off all week about wasting money . . . behaving like a floozy . . getting above her station.

Louise was beaming. 'I'm so glad you have come after all. I was afraid you wouldn't. I know it's a long way.' She began pouring tea into fragile rose-painted china which the maid had brought in, handing a cup to Emily who was almost afraid to grasp the handle in case it came away in her fingers.

'There are three others to come,' Louise went on. 'Una and Maude Holiday and Mrs Jane Barrat. Do you know them?'

Emily shook her head, wanting desperately to ask if her bicycle was really all right and if she could go and see it. She had dreamed about it every night that week. But Louise was chattering on about the coming ride, explaining the route.

'There will be people enjoying Sunday leisure in the suburbs so they are bound to see a group of female cyclists. After all, the important thing is to be noticed and have the placards read.' She waited, eyebrows slightly raised as if inviting comment.

Words receded further back in Emily's mind. To cover her embarrassment she gulped the tea, choked and spluttered violently. As Vera patted her back, she wished she had never come. It was going to be a series of increasingly awkward situations, she could feel it in her bones. In the middle of her convulsion the door opened and the maid announced:

'The Misses Una and Maude Holiday.'

Emily wiped her streaming eyes and was confronted by the brown velvet sisters who had abandoned their discreet dresses for daring navy-blue bloomers. She knew she was staring, but couldn't take her eyes off such a remarkable sight. Vera sat neat and straight in her chair, very prim, small mouth pulled up tight with disapproval.

Louise introduced everyone and dispensed tea, listening with a slight frown to the excuses Una brought from Mrs Barrat.

'Her eldest boy is ill again.'

'Again?' There was a hint of irritation in the way Louise spoke.

'He does suffer from his asthma,' Una added.

Louise put down her cup. 'Perhaps. But I'm more inclined to think it is yet another instance of cold feet.

However, there's nothing more to say. When you have all finished your tea we might as well go and collect our bicycles as there is no one else to come.'

They filed into the hall, waited while Jones fetched Louise's coat, then followed her through the front door, down shallow stone steps on to a gravelled path bordering the house. Looking up again at the red and blue brick crust of turrets, pinnacles and gargoyles, Emily thought the whole thing looked like a Bath bun gone mad. There must be dozens of rooms. All that cleaning! Not that they lacked servants to do it. Why would a person like Louise Marshall bother her head about Votes for Women when it was obvious she had everything money could buy?

They walked in two groups. Louise and the sisters in front, laughing and chatting easily – Vera and Emily behind, subdued; diffident.

In spite of everything Louise had talked about, they had nothing in common except their sex. The stirring speech seemed unreal and far away. A heap of dry words, like the wind-blown leaves trapped under the box hedges edging the path. You only had to look at the neat rows of wallflowers, or the cut of the clothes of the three in front, to know equality was all eyewash. It was a daft notion, talking about everyone having the same opportunities. Men didn't, so women hadn't a hope. And if that was the truth, why was she here? It was a hopeless muddle. At least her bicycle was real, and there it was!

Emily caught her breath as Louise led them into a paved yard surrounded by stables. She had eyes for nothing but her beautiful bicycle, shining like the day it had first come out of a shop. There was not a mark, not a scratch to be seen and the wheels and handlebars shot sparks of silver in the sunshine.

'Pleased?' Peter Marshall uncurled from beneath the bonnet of his car which was parked in the middle of the yard.

Emily gulped, unable to say anything at all.

'Just gave it a touch of paint once I'd finished the repairs. Gardiner restrung the broken strings for you.' He indicated a wiry little man who was doubled up over the car engine.

Emily forced out: 'Thanks!' feeling suddenly very friendly towards this former antagonist.

'I've got the placards stacked in the stable here,' Louise said.

There were five other bicycles propped at intervals along the stable walls. Emily realized none of them was as immaculate as her own. She grasped the handlebars and wheeled it a short distance, just to convince herself that this splendid object was really hers.

Louise came out of the stable carrying some pieces of cardboard pasted over with white paper and boldly lettered in green: 'VOTES FOR WOMEN'.

'Pete, be a dear and fix these for me.'

Peter, who had gone back to the car, straightened up again. He said tartly: 'What's happened to your principles? I thought women were able to cope with anything just as well as, if not better than, mere men!'

'Of course they are, but we're all ready to set off,' as if the job would dirty their clothes.

'Well it's no use going without the placards,' Peter said, and turned back to the car.

Louise was nettled. 'Very well . . . don't help then! Give me some pliers . . . and what have you done with the garden wire? It isn't on the hook any more.'

For the third time Peter stood up. 'Oh for goodness sake, Lou, I'll do it!' He disappeared into one of the stables and reappeared with a coil of wire. Emily watched him deftly secure a placard to the handlebars and frame of each bicycle, coming to hers last. Understanding his irritation, she said:

'I'll do mine.'

He hesitated. 'It's all right . . . don't take any notice of me. I was only ribbing her.'

'Yo was right. We should help ourselves.'

He looked at her, approving the determination in her round dark eyes and the jut of her chin. There was determination in the way she carried her strong body as well;

and an unexpected country vitality in her broad apple cheeks and upward curling mouth. Giving her the pliers and wire, he said softly:

'A vote for this woman!'

Emily was glad to be busy, making holes in the cardboard, threading the wire through and winding it round handlebars and frame. She was able to hide her red face. The open confidence of his gaze had made her hot. She was suddenly aware that his composure, the certainty with which he did everything, possessed a power she had never known before. Although his remark confused her and she quickly turned away to join the others, she felt the day had gained a purpose.

A comradeship flowered as they left the yard and wheeled their bicycles down the drive and out into the tree-lined road. They were drawn together by the tension of being exposed to the public eye, although the road was empty. Emily sat on the saddle, wondering nervously if she would still be able to balance. The placard resisted the mild wind and made guiding the bicycle difficult. She wobbled, swerved and nearly collided with Vera, but struggled to stay on and finally succeeded in steering a fairly straight course. They reached the end of the road where houses thinned and country took over.

'Mind the potholes,' Louise shouted too late.

Emily bumped over what seemed like a small crater, almost came to grief, but zigzagged to victory on the opposite side of the road. Her hands were slimy with sweat, slipping on the hard grips, but she was absolutely determined not to give in.

The sun shining through a network of branches made a moving pattern on the ground and over their bodies, like golden water. The scent of wet grass, the sunlight, the meadows spread out either side of the road, insisted on raising Emily's spirits. It was easier riding now, with confidence coming back. Her fears receded as they left Hardwick behind, but when the houses reappeared so did feelings of apprehension. They were all aware of it. More houses meant more people. A number were out for a Sunday stroll and several stopped to stare and point.

'Just what we want,' Louise called. 'We need to be a circus act – doesn't matter if they laugh, so long as we're noticed. Mrs Pankhurst's right. It's no good patiently waiting, hoping someone will take pity and listen to respectable pleas. That's the way to be ignored. *Do* something . . . anything so long as it's outrageous enough. Then the papers will report. A few bold headlines are worth a hundred letters to Members of Parliament.'

Emily felt sure Louise was right, but a large part of her shrank from the idea of being on show. The sisters were an attraction in Louise's terms. Too much so for Emily's comfort, though the feeling left her sneakingly ashamed. She and Louise were cycling side by side now as the road curved right and gardens telescoped into green patches in front of terraced houses.

Emily concentrated hard on the road. She could hear the others throwing remarks with occasional giggles, but she didn't want to look up. Street after street and hardly one that didn't harbour sharp-tongued comment or ribald laughter.

'What's your hubby doing, letting yo out on your own?' . . . 'Should be home taking care of the kids and the cat!' . . . 'A strong man 'ud put some sense into them scatter-brained heads; warm them backsides an' all!' . . . 'Stupid crazy women – yo're all stupid crazy women – we don't want none of your sort round here – they do right to lock yo up – whipping's what yo need – bloody crazy women!' . . . But it was mostly good-natured. Only one other, this time an elderly gentleman, looked really outraged and deliberately urged his dog to chase after them. It was a fat dog and couldn't last the pace, but it was unnerving and Emily was glad when both were out of sight. Louise went pedalling on apparently enjoying the stir which set Emily's insides curdling, and when an old woman waved a feather duster and shouted:

'Go it, gels . . . the best of luck!' from her bedroom window, Louise called back: 'Women for ever . . . Votes for Women!'

The whole episode was taking on a theatrical quality. The new bicycle, the strange company, the crazy thing they were doing, made Emily feel like someone else. Her old self had been left back in the kitchen at home along with the washing-up. She was Lady-in-Waiting to Queen Louise. The side street joined with a narrower one. Louise had already taken the right-hand turn, Una and Maude behind. Emily, followed by Vera, swept after them.

'Cor . . . look at that!'

A group of lads out for an afternoon walk, showing off their finery, very dandy with bowler hats and walking sticks. But the burst of laughter was less for Emily than Una and Maude. The first youth grabbed his companion.

'Link arms!' he shouted.

Louise was leading, but before she could ride past the danger-point they had spread across the road. She braked hard and almost fell, skirts wrapping round her legs.

'Look here!' one of them said. 'We've nobbled some of those Suffragettes.' He came closer, poking at the placard and making a jagged tear in the paper.

'Now look what you've done,' snapped Louise.

'Watch yourself, Fred. The lady's a redhead, temper to match I shouldn't wonder.'

'I can manage a spitfire like her!' Fred was all confidence, upturned nose, bouncy curls.

'Fancy her, do you?'

'I'd rather have one of those two,' shouted a small dark lad who was trying very hard to grow a beard and moustache. 'They were in such a hurry they forgot to finish dressing . . . came out in their drawers!'

'Bloomers to you,' Maude said with great dignity.

'And fly-buttons to you, miss!' He raised his bowler.

Emily wanted to laugh and lash out at the same time. She measured the situation, noting how they were closing in. Five against five and they were bigger, but if they really tried anything she'd give them a bashing they wouldn't forget. There were one or two tricks she had learned from the occasional Saturday night brawls that overflowed from the pub.

'Stand aside!' Louise commanded, with enough authority to make them hesitate.

To Emily's relief Peter chose that moment to drive the

Maudslay round the corner beyond the shops, coming towards them. From the other end of the street a brougham appeared at a brisk pace. The appearance of the two vehicles seemed to demoralize the youths. They wandered back on to the pavement continuing their stroll with only an occasional backward glance.

'Trouble?' Peter asked, leaning out as he drew up beside them.

'Nothing worth a mention,' Louise said scornfully.

'Picnic time then, girls. Only another half-mile to go. Race you!'

'Idiot!' Louise laughed. 'You know we haven't a hope of winning. You can set everything out ready.' She shouted as the car rolled away: 'And don't eat anything till we get there.'

The picnic site was under a large oak tree at the top of a gently sloping field. The smoke and dust of Birmingham lay behind them; in front, stretching to the horizon, the browning shades of autumn country. A few late swallows dipped, broke away, only to circle again. Leaning back against the trunk of the tree Emily revelled in stillness. The effort of cycling had been greater than she had realized. Peter was passing plates and packages to Louise who was kneeling by a white cloth spread over the grass. It was all so peaceful . . . still as odd as a dream with Una and Maude in their music-hall bloomers hugging their knees, and Vera unbending enough to say she hadn't enjoyed anything so much, not in ages.

Sandwiches distributed, Louise stretched and said: 'This is such a marvellous change from being bored . . . you wouldn't believe! I sometimes think women aren't expected to have minds at all. We're supposed to be servants and baby-making machines. What a prospect!'

Peter, lying full length on the grass, hands behind his head, rolled over on one elbow. 'That's a gloomy picture.'

'No one said it wasn't. It *is* gloomy . . . like something out of the underworld.'

'Exaggeration.'

'No it's not . . . you agree, don't you?' she appealed to the others.

49

The new person who had entered Emily said: 'It's the truth. Only thing wrong is it don't say it all . . . not the dreariness.'

Louise was touched by this hint of real involvement. 'You *do* care . . . about how things are for women.'

'Course I do. How can yo live it and not care!' Emily was amazing herself by being so fervent, but knew she meant every word. 'Yo talks like a dream and don't yo let anyone tell yo different. Yo made it clear to me. I felt them things before . . . slavery and being treated like so much dirt, but I couldn't put no name to it.'

'Emily Palmer, I like you. I can see we are going to get on like a house on fire.'

They looked at one another in a way that made Emily's skin tingle.

'So long as we don't have to burn none to prove it,' she said, surprising herself again.

Louise broke into a shower of irresistible laughter, easing the tension, but destroying none of the joy. 'Now who has the silver tongue!'

'Not me,' Emily assured her, feeling as if they had been friends for years. 'Yo'd never guess I hankered to be a teacher, would yo? But what 'ud be the good . . . words running every which way. Now yo *could* be one – a real corker.'

'Only one snag – I don't like children. Squalling little brats, most of them.' Louise pulled a face. 'No, I shan't be a teacher and I shan't be married either. Just imagine facing half a dozen jammy faces round the breakfast table every morning!'

'Yo don't have to have children,' Emily ventured.

'And that's another thing. Try explaining how to avoid it.'

There was a distinct silence. In her new role, Emily found enough courage to look for each person's reaction. Peter, chewing on a grass stalk, was looking quizzical. Una and Maude were obviously embarrassed. Vera, whom she had expected to look shocked, showed nothing but a trace of sadness. She was a queer one. In the three years they had worked together for Ma Harris she'd learned almost nothing about her. And Vic knew precious little more. She'd come closer to Louise in these last few minutes than all that time with Vera.

Peter got up. 'After that little pearl, I think this is the moment for treats. Bubbly, girls. Get your glasses.'

Champagne! Whatever would Mam think if she knew?

Louise said loudly: 'I intend to devote my life to the Cause, like Christabel and Mrs P.'

'Who's Christabel?' Emily asked.

Peter groaned. 'Don't let's get started on *that*.'

Louise looked at him frostily. 'I think we should drink a toast to Christabel – Mrs Pankhurst's eldest daughter and our second-in-command. She's a jewel . . . a diamond . . .'

'Lou,' Peter said gently, 'cut out the eulogies. You aren't on the platform. It's playtime, remember?'

Louise turned on him. 'Playtime . . . that's you to a tee. Never think of anything serious. Life is a series of frolics, like those stupid balloons.'

'At least I don't go round dropping conversational bricks right and left.'

'Oh shut up, Pete! You really are a monumental bore sometimes.'

From banter the exchange had become a battle. Emily looked from one to the other, afraid of the childish truculence on their faces; so ridiculously similar.

'Meaning what?' Peter asked with a dangerous edge to his voice.

'Meaning exactly that.'

'Useful only as a handyman for fixing placards on bikes, running errands, acting as chauffeur, provider of picnics?'

'Absolutely right . . . on the nail. Now will you let me finish what I was going to say?'

'Once you set your mind on talking, no one, not even God, could stop you!'

'Don't blaspheme!'

They really were like a couple of kids. If they went on like this all the time, what a load of useless words they must have spread around in their lives.

'I'm sure he didn't really mean . . .' Una began with

ill-timed good intention.

'Oh yes he did!' Louise said.

Peter didn't reply. Putting down his glass and the bottle, he picked up his cap, placed it firmly on his head, climbed over the gate and went through the ritual of starting the car. Emily watched, appalled at the way the happiness was falling to pieces. She willed Louise to call out an apology, but she didn't. There was no side to be on now they were both her friends. How could they ruin everything for no real reason at all?

The car drove off, sudden acceleration sending up a shower of little stones and dust particles. In a moment it had vanished beyond the curve in the lane, leaving a group of forlorn bicycles leaning against the hedge; taking the laughter out of the day.

5

EMILY opened the door of Mrs Harris's Dressmaking Establishment and found Louise on the doorstep, just as she had done before Christmas, but this time there was something different about her. Emily stood back to let her pass, curiously stirred by the impact of seeing her after so many weeks.

'Oh I'm glad it's you,' Louise said. 'I want some help. It's important. Is there somewhere we can talk privately?'

Emily closed the door, but not before she had glimpsed the Maudslay drawing away from the kerb. She saw Peter Marshall, but he was frowning as he stared through the windscreen and he didn't wave or smile. There was no real reason why he should, but all the same she sensed that something was wrong-side out.

'What is it? Tell me quick before we go up to the fitting-room, or Mrs Harris will wonder why we're being so long.'

But Louise was afraid of being overheard. 'Let's go in there.' She indicated the parlour. Reluctantly Emily followed. Inside the room, Louise caught hold of her hands, urgency flowing like an electric force.

'We've got to do something positive. Make a stand. Show them we're not to be trifled with.'

Emily was confused. 'Who?'

'You *are* with me, aren't you? I mean, I can trust you?'

With those beautiful eyes entreating her and the thrilling pressure of Louise's hands, how could she refuse? Emily felt as if the whole of her mind had been captured. It was not so much the meaning of Louise's words as her manner, that was the magnet. When she turned the full force of her personality on you there was no way of resisting. But she didn't want to resist. She was a willing prisoner.

'Of course yo can. But I don't understand . . .' How

beautiful she was; little tendrils of hair escaping from beneath her large yellow hat; soft yellow dress under a bronze twill coat. Golden!

'I've thought of a plan, but I can't do it alone. I'm sick to death of all these useless meetings. You've been to some so you know what they're like – nothing but words . . . words . . . words. We need action if we're ever going to get the Vote. People take notice of action, especially drastic action.'

In spite of the wholehearted response being drawn out of Emily a small wisp of caution remained. 'What sort of things was yo thinking of?'

'We should take a leaf out of Mrs Pankhurst's book.'

'Break windows, yo means?' Emily was alarmed . . . excited.

Louise tightened her grip. 'No . . . I had something else in mind.'

'What then?' If she didn't spit it out soon, Ma Harris would be down and then there'd be trouble. She'd already asked a few difficult questions about the meeting at the Vicarage. If it hadn't been held in such a respectable place, there might have been trouble. Her manner had said as much. As for the bicycle parade . . . and those bloomers . . . Emily sweated at the thought. She couldn't afford to lose her job. And if Dad was to find out she'd gone against him after all he'd said about the bicycle parade, he'd wallop her from one end of Birmingham to the other. All this weighed on her mind, but at the same time she was caught and held in a web of passionate admiration for Louise, so her will became a helpless yielding thing.

'Promise you won't let me down?' Louise begged.

The warmth of her grip almost burned. Emily felt the last drop of caution dissolve. None of her thoughts was coherent and she drowned in a tide of unrecognizable emotions that came rushing through her body. Words refused to form and all she could do was nod.

'It will have to be at night. That's the only time no one will be about,' Louise said, as if she had already explained her plan. 'Your part is this . . . I want you to get hold of

54

some lengths of material, green, purple and white. Can you do that?'

Emily found her voice. 'I don't know. There might be some scraps, but Mrs Harris is that mingy, she don't give much away.'

'Oh well, it doesn't matter. I'll buy some and give it to you. Probably be the best thing in the long run. Less likely to be found out. It's the sewing I want you to do. I'm hopeless. We'll need eighteen flags altogether . . . striped with the three colours. How fast can you make them?'

'Depends how early we get let out. We sometimes have to work late when there's a rush job. It's busy now with Easter trade building up.' Was it to be some kind of demonstration – flag-waving?

'Wednesday today . . . say Saturday night, or Sunday?'

There was a kind of wildness about Louise that kindled an answering abandon in Emily. To hell with her drab constricting life . . . whatever the consequences!

'Better say Sunday.' It would be difficult enough. She'd have to sit up late – sneak a candle from Ma Harris's store in her kitchen dresser. There were none to spare at home. May might help. She was deft with a needle.

They heard the stairs creak under heavy feet. Ma Harris screeched:

'Emily, where have you got to?'

'I'm for it now,' Emily whispered.

Louise gave her hands a little shake before letting go. 'Don't worry, I'll soon settle *her*,' calling out: 'In here, Mrs Harris. I was just showing Emily some of the styles in this magazine. There's a delightful dress and jacket which caught my fancy.'

The door was pushed open, but before Mrs Harris came into view, Louise muttered: 'Tonight at six-thirty. I'll be waiting for you . . . Oh, good afternoon, Mrs Harris,' with the melting charm of her smile.

'Miss Marshall, I'm sorry you've been kept waiting down here. Miss Palmer should have brought you straight up to the fitting-room.'

Under the suspicious eye of Ma Harris, Emily felt vulnerable, as if her thoughts were on display for anyone to read. She was thankful to return to the workroom. But it was no escape.

'Who came?' Alice mumbled, her mouth full of pins.

'Miss Marshall,' Emily sat down and picked up the shot-silk taffeta she had been working on.

'Oo, 'er! My auntie says she's a real little bitch. Treats 'er dad like dirt. Doesn't take a bit of notice of anything 'e says.'

Emily didn't want to talk, but this attack on Louise was more than she could bear. 'What's your auntie know about it?'

'She's got a friend that lives 'Ardwick way . . . does charring at My Lady Marshall's 'ouse,' Alice said.

'Well I've been there and it ain't true,' Emily retorted, and then regretted letting slip this connection with Louise.

Flo giggled. 'Hark at our Emmie! Go on then, yo can't stop now. Tell us why yo went.'

Emily drew long tacking stitches through the whispering taffeta, hating the interest she had aroused, calling herself all sorts of a fool. Vera had more sense, quietly sewing at the table under the window, her back to the others, minding her own business. Why couldn't she learn to be like Vera? Holding herself in, all secret. If she stole the crown jewels, no one would find out.

'Go on, Emmie . . . tell us . . .'

But she didn't have to after all because Ma Harris came stumping up the stairs, Louise following. As they crossed the workroom Emily bent over her work, cheeks aflame, not daring to look up. The room was full of Louise; scent and sound of her. More than that . . . But Emily could not define, only feel it in the tingling of her nerves and the way her heart thumped. Was it less than three months since she had been knocked off her bicycle into a whole new world? It was more thrilling than that visit to the pantomime last year when May had laughed herself silly over the Dame falling into a bucket of whitewash. It was good seeing May laugh. Warming and cosy. Not like now. These whirling sensations smacked of danger. But hadn't she been crying out for change? You couldn't play at escaping without danger. In and out, in and out with these wretched tackings, Flo giggling under her breath, Ada and Alice whispering as they appliquéd sprays of silver flowers on a white satin ball gown. Mrs Craig would look a fright – mutton dressed as lamb.

'Thank you, Mrs Harris. I'm delighted with the pattern . . . delighted. Next Tuesday, you say?' Louise came sweeping from the fitting-room. This time their eyes met. A wink and she was gone, sending Emily, about turn, back into that earthquake of toppling emotions.

'Emily, you're forgetting your hat!'

'Oh . . . thanks!' Emily took the battered felt from Vera. It was after half past six already, nearly seven and she didn't know where Louise would be waiting, if she had bothered to stay on.

Vera watched her wordlessly.

The others were chattering as they got ready to go home.

'Oo, my behind . . . I'm that stiff with sitting . . .'

'Yo coming, Flo?'

'Turn the gas down, love, if yo're last out . . .' They scuttled about gathering last-minute belongings. 'Night, Emmie! Night, Vera!'

In spite of her anxiety to be gone, Emily dawdled, wanting to be the last away, so that she could look for Louise without awkward questions. But Vera seemed to be taking her time. Twice she glanced at Emily as if weighing up something in her mind; on the point of speech. Emily refolded the taffeta in its calico wrapping, dropped a thimble into the drawer, then gave up and went out into the passage.

'Good night, Emily. Left the gas burning, have you?'

'Vera's just turning it down, Mrs Harris.'

'That's all right then. Mind you pull the door to properly.'

'Yes, Mrs Harris.' Old cow! She was so thrifty she'd catch herself coming in on the way out if she wasn't careful!

Out in the street Vic was leaning against a gaslamp, his breath clouding in the frosty air. Vera came up behind. Emily was trapped between them; and no sign of Louise.

'I was on my way home,' Vic said casually. 'Thought I'd wait for yo. Give us your basket.' He took it from Vera, who was silent as usual. 'How's things at work? Busy are yo?' Vic was trying to push the conversation along without much result. Ordinarily Emily would have joined in, but tonight she was preoccupied. They walked along the cramped pavement, Vic slightly behind. 'Talk of a strike at the works,' he went on undaunted. 'Gaffers want something for nothing like always. We only asked for a few pence more and they're up in arms. Same old story.'

'Us and them,' Vera said suddenly. She smiled at Vic.

Like the sun breaking through clouds, Emily thought, surprised from her own troubles. Vic was encouraged to take Vera's arm.

'I'll walk yo back to your lodgings,' he offered.

'Yo do that,' Emily said, glad of an escape. 'See yo tomorrer, Vera.'

They had reached the end of the street and had seen only a rag and bone man with his cart. Emily was in despair. She watched Vera and Vic cross over and turn down the alley past the school. The night was empty and even the crystal stars had a hard look strung up there in all that black velvet. No use hanging around. Ma Harris would be having a sly peep through her net curtains with those opera glasses a customer had passed on. The pub was doing good trade judging from the noise. She could do with something to warm her. Insides clapped together like ice-cold slate. Not hungry . . . empty. She paused at the crossroads gazing hopelessly along the dismal streets in turn. A few people were hurrying home, anxious to get out of the raw March night. Only a tramp took his time, slouching past, a bundle of stinking rags, cardboard tied under his flapping shoes in a pathetic attempt to keep out the damp.

And then, when she had given up all hope, the Marshalls' car came slowly round a corner fifty yards beyond the pub and halted under a streetlamp. The murky light was enough to show Peter and Louise talking. Emily sprinted across the cobbles, her throat tight, heart hammering. Then stopped. They weren't talking, they were quarrelling again. Indistinguishable words rushed at her. She didn't know whether to walk on and pretend not to notice the row or turn back. No, she couldn't do that. Suddenly Louise opened the car door and got out, slamming it behind her.

'I dare you!' she said loudly and marched towards Emily, grabbing her arms in a grip that was almost painful. 'They shan't stop me,' she said with so much imprisoned anger that Emily felt quite frightened. Louise smiled, anger apparently melting as rapidly as it had come. Except for the tight hold on her arms Emily would have thought it had vanished altogether. She could feel a violence in Louise potentially more dangerous than any of Mam's outbursts or Dad's drunken ravings.

'What must you think,' Louise began. 'It's just . . . oh, MEN! But never mind that now.' She glanced over her shoulder at the Maudslay which was moving slowly towards them. Lowering her voice she said: 'I don't want Pete to hear.' She shook Emily as if to force in the intensity of her words. 'You won't let me down?'

'Of course not.' She would die for her.

'It has to be at night. We will go to the golf course at Hardwick and replace all the flags on the greens with the ones you make, then we are going to paint VOTES FOR WOMEN in huge letters on the grass all the way round each one in whitewash. Now which night can you be ready?'

For a blank moment Emily stared at her. The anticlimax was so great she would have burst out laughing if Louise hadn't retained such a tight hold. The idea might be funny, but Louise was deadly serious and to even hint that she saw it that way would destroy the bond between them for ever and she couldn't bear that. Besides, there was danger in it. You couldn't go round messing about with other people's property without stirring up trouble, so it was more than just a game. All the same, some of the glamour had been rubbed off, but none of the fear.

Peter brought the car to a standstill beside the kerb. Emily glanced sideways at him with a ghost of a smile and was given a nod that barely disguised his black mood.

'I've a package for you,' Louise said, opening the car door as if everything was perfectly normal.

Emily guessed it to be the lengths of cloth for the flags. She took the brown paper parcel.

'You'll have the blouse ready by next Sunday without fail, won't you?'

'Yes, Miss Marshall.' It was like acting in a play. A mad game. At least it added a bit of spice to the dreary routine.

'As for the trimmings,' Louise went on. 'Let me see . . . six buttons . . .' She took a small notebook with a little pencil suspended from it by a tasselled cord from her coat pocket, wrote in it, then tore out the page and gave it to Emily. Before there was time to read the message she had climbed back into the car and, with a wave, was driven away.

Emily looked at the scrap of paper. 'SUNDAY NEXT. Midnight. Will wait at the bottom of the drive – Tower House. Bring flags.'

Without the hypnotic effect of Louise's presence, doubt attacked her again. What if they were caught? They might be arrested! And how would Mam and Dad take that? Neighbours accepted men rolling home of a Saturday night: family rowing: the occasional fight. But a girl standing up for Women's Rights . . . worse still, tangling with the bobbies . . . She'd be tipped out of home! The nip of frost on her fingers seemed more real than Louise's wild schemes. She was in half a mind not to go. And yet to let Louise down . . . Not that!

Still puzzling, Emily opened the back door.

'Shut that bloody door, can't yo? There's a draught like a cut-throat razor.'

Dad was hunched in the wooden armchair. With her back to him, Mam was by the range putting all her feelings into stirring a pan of broth. The atmosphere was thick with trouble.

Not wanting to add fuel, Emily said: 'Sorry, Dad,' and

slipped hastily through into the passage to hang up her coat.

All week there had been tension. Much more than usual.

'Give us a hand, Emmie.' May was coming down the stairs on her bottom.

'What's up?' Emily asked her as she half-carried her the rest of the way. 'Mam's scowling fit for slaughter, and Dad's scratchy.'

'Don't know.' May looked unhappy. 'I went upstairs to get out of the way. Miss Barnes lent me a lovely story to read today. She says I can keep it as long as I like. But I have to give it back before I leave school.'

And that would be Easter time. Mam had already arranged with Mrs Harris to take her on for a pittance to learn the dressmaking trade. It wasn't fair when she so loved her books. Emily gave her a squeeze.

'Yo been reading by streetlight again? Yo'll hurt your eyes.'

She heard the back door slam and the rumble of Ernie's voice. Mam called out for her to come and make herself useful.

'I'll need a clean shirt for tonight,' Ernie said as Emily went back into the kitchen. 'There's a special meeting been called up at the Chapel. I'm speaking.'

'Well I'm not bloody ironing it! As if I've not enough on my plate, cooking and cleaning for the lot of yo.' Mam stirred hard and broth slopped on to the range, giving off an acrid smoky smell.

'Our Emmie can do it,' Ernie said.

'I've other chores,' Emily snapped.

Mam turned, glaring. 'Yo do it, girl, when yo're asked.'

'Why should I?' Caught out by indignation, Emily spoke without thinking.

'Because I'm telling yo, that's why. And if yo don't like it yo knows what yo can do.'

'But that's not fair . . .' An unnamed force drove Emily towards the brink of disaster.

'Not fair . . . I'll give yo not fair!' Mam shouted, batting at her with the hot spoon out of the broth.

'Can't yo bloody shut up? Yammering on like a pair

of alley cats,' Dad bellowed into the middle of the argument. 'Where's my supper? I've been out breaking my back all day and comes home to a lot of screeching women!'

All the cloudy doubts that had been gnawing Emily on the way home suddenly vanished. I'll do it . . . I'll go! Nothing shall stop me. At least the madness of decorating a golf course with whitewash and flags was better than the madness at home.

6

THE night was bitingly cold. Emily buried the tip of her nose farther under the bedclothes. The idea of getting up, dressing, then creeping out of the house and riding her bicycle all the way to Hardwick was appalling. But she couldn't back out now. No, not couldn't . . . wouldn't! Whatever was the time? A ribbon of white moonlight lay across the blanket, rippling as May turned in her sleep. Emily strained to distinguish the snores drifting in. Low and rhythmic, Vic; sharp snores, Ernie; Dad's house-shakers. But there was no way of telling whether Mam was asleep. It must be after eleven now. Half an hour needed to cycle the four miles. She would just have to risk it. Cautiously she shifted to the edge of the bed and pushed back the bedding. Thank goodness she had left most of her clothes on under her nightdress. Shivering, she fumbled with the buttons on her dress, then scrabbled under the bed for her boots and the flags which were wrapped in a parcel. As she pulled it out the paper scratched on the lino.

'Is it tonight, Emmie?' May whispered.

'I thought yo was asleep.' Emily got off her knees and put the bundle on the bed. 'I should've put these in something that didn't rustle.'

'Wish I could come.' May knew all about the scheme. Emily leaned over and kissed her. 'Yo're in the best place. It's could enough to freeze the whiskers off a cat!'

'I want to *do* something too.'

'Yo have. Think of all those flags yo sewed. I'd never have got them ready if it hadn't been for you!' Emily felt warmer, seeing her smile. 'I'll be back before anyone's up.' Please God let this be true, she prayed, and taking the parcel and her boots, she blew another kiss and crept out of the room.

There were a thousand new creaks in the stairboards and she almost dropped the parcel trying to step quietly. She must have been mad not to leave it under the sacks with the bicycle. In the kitchen an eye of red squinted between the bars of the range, last embers of the fire. Not enough to boil a kettle even if she had time. A hot drink would have put her right for the journey. Never mind, she'd warm up if she pedalled hard. She put on her boots and coat, winding a long muffler round her head and neck. The bolts on the back door were stiff and only yielded when she jerked at them. In an agony of apprehension she opened the door which had developed a special night squeak. Surely Mam with her bat's ears would have heard? But she dare not wait to find out. A gust of icy wind caught her throat, making her gasp as she went into the yard. If it got a mite warmer there'd be snow. Peeling off the sacks she carefully moved Vic's bicycle, then her own, replacing Vic's under the sacks before tying the parcel under the saddle. Wheeling the bicycle down the entry she experienced the same thrill which came every time she touched it. If she lived to be a hundred it would always be like that, she was sure of it.

Out in the street bright moonlight, eclipsing the dim gaslighting, picked diamonds from the frosty cobbles. She got on her bicycle, a little scared by the film of ice that crackled underfoot. It would have to be a very careful ride. No giving way to the thrill of speed or she'd find herself in a nasty crumpled heap. Thank God there were no people about, not even the hint of anyone still out of bed.

Pedalling was no substitute for fire, a hot drink or the comforts of her stone hot water-bottle. Her feet were frozen, though her body felt warm enough. As for her fingers, the only way she could tell she still had any was by an aching numbness, in spite of two pairs of Vic's old socks she was wearing as gloves. Behind her, the parcel crackled. Under the bicycle wheels ice hissed. Sharp hard sounds. Rooftops, factory chimneys, church spires, cut into the steely skyline. No breath of softness to be found. Even the wind stabbed and pierced with needle-sharpness. Familiar streets changed and took on the unreal quality of stiff photographs. She was cycling through a dream landscape that shrivelled her courage and took away her sense of direction.

'Dafty!' she said aloud to break the spell. 'Born and bred in Brum and scared by a bit of moonlight!' She was not impressed by her own scorn, but it did something towards bringing back a sense of reality, and when a pair of cats split the air with their child's cries she was startled, but able to keep on going.

The city centre was behind her now, as she worked through back streets avoiding any chance of being observed. A train whistle shrieked and the steady clanking of goods vans echoed clearly through the night hush. A few city lights sparkled; Snow Hill station; New Street. Once or twice distant figures emerged from the gloom, but they disappeared into side streets before she reached them. Strange how a city never seemed entirely asleep. As she moved through the subdued streets unchallenged, courage and warmth began slowly trickling back. It was going to be all right after all. She was through the worst and would soon reach the narrow fringe of fields separating Hardwick from Birmingham. Ahead was a wider road, peppered with shops. Sailing into it with her rediscovered courage she was horrified to see a policeman walking purposefully towards her. He came out of the shadows into a pool of lamplight, a solid unavoidable figure, hands clasped behind his back. There was no hope of retreat. She had been seen. The only thing to do was put on a bold front. If only her legs and arms would behave!

'Cold night to be out, miss,' the constable said, as they came nearer. 'Late, too.' There was no mistaking the question in his voice.

She was not going to stop. He could hardly leap out and grab her, or sprint after her if she kept on going.

'Sharp frost,' she remarked, wishing her voice wouldn't shake. 'I'll be glad to get home.'

He smiled, nodding . . . and she was past!

'Good night, miss.'

'Good night.' Would he remember the encounter when the news of the golf course attack spread the next day? But even if he did, she was well muffled. There was no way he could recognize her again. The thought gave her no peace of mind, and by the time she arrived at the Tower House the only thing that had any meaning was her promise to Louise not to betray her trust.

'I thought you'd never get here!' Louise came out of the shadows by the big iron gates. 'You're late.'

'I'm sorry! I couldn't leave home before everyone was asleep.'

'Oh, it doesn't matter. Have you got the flags?'

'Yes.' Indicating the bundle.

'I've got scissors and brushes. The can of whitewash is under that bush. Shove your bike in here. You can lean it on that tree. That's right. We'll walk the rest of the way. It's not far.'

Under the moon's light, Louise looked pallid. A white disc of a face swathed in a dark hood. Dark clothes. Both of them alike. Conspirators! They walked away from the house along the broad road in silence, except for the clicking of their heels.

'This way,' Louise said.

The lane was narrow. A country way with grass verges and high-banked hedges that cut out all but a thin strip of light. The gloom seemed to relieve some tension in Louise. She began talking in a low voice.

'If you hadn't come I was going to paint the greens alone. I have to do something you see . . . *have* to.'

'Why is it so important?' Emily asked.

'Isn't it important to you?' Louise sounded surprised.

'Yes, but . . .' She was groping after the real root cause for Louise's sudden switch from the routine of drawing-room meetings to secret adventures in the middle of the night.

'I met someone,' Louise replied to her unformed question. 'Mary Grant. She came up from London to speak at one of our drawing-room meetings. It was incredible listening to her. She has been in Holloway prison four times and she described the way she was forcibly fed. Oh – it is monstrous – disgusting! I don't know how she could have borne it, she is so frail and delicate, like a tiny bird. But she's got the courage of a lion.'

Emily shivered, recognizing the undercurrent of violence in Louise's voice again.

'Those prison doctors are brutes. Some of the things Mary said made me want to vomit . . .'

Emily was afraid Louise was going to describe the scenes in detail and hastily interrupted. 'She must be brave.'

'She is . . . but there are many others and they're all prepared to go back again and again even though it means going through the whole ghastly business once more.' Louise sounded almost as if she were enjoying the horror.

'Would you do it? Go on hunger strike, I mean?' asked Emily.

Louise did not answer straight away and when she did, sounded uncertain.

'I believe I could. Thinking about it now, in the open air, it would be easy to say "Of course". But it's when you are there, shut away inside the prison that counts. It will all be different then.'

Will be? She made it sound as if this was waiting for them just round the corner, an inevitable happening. 'Yo really mean that,' Emily said slowly. The implications were enormous. 'Are yo going to keep on doing things like tonight?'

'This is just the beginning. You'll see!'

'Mary Grant must have been a real soul-mover,' Emily said with conviction.

'She is. Hearing her tipped the scales.'

So there *was* something else. Before she could probe further Louise touched her arm.

'There's a cart track here. If we go up it there are two gates, one on each side. They lead on to the golf course. It spreads out either side. Used to be farm land, you see. The farmhouse is still there, just at the top of this track.'

'Does anyone live there?'

'Oh yes. The farmer has land the other side of the course.'

Then there were people near by; dogs perhaps. Emily tied up the remains of her courage. She'd come this far. It was no use getting cold feet now. Cold feet? Hers were freezing! 'Let's get a move on, before we turn into snowmen. Yo go first and tell me what to do.' It occurred to her that she had no idea what a green was, had never seen a golf course. All she knew of golf were some strange pictures she had seen in a magazine.

They left the track, edging through the swing gate into rough grass. The ground was hard and lumpy beneath their feet. The full moonlight revealed the land falling away into a shallow valley, to rise against a horizon that was broken by the dark bunching of trees and bushes.

'Down here,' Louise whispered.

Rime flicked from long grass blades as they tramped downhill to a flat, closely-mown lawn which had a flag on a pole sticking out of the ground. So *that* was the purpose of the flags she had stitched. Eighteen! They'd have to work fast or it would be daylight before they finished.

'Here!' Louise handed her a pair of scissors. 'Cut off the old flags and tie on one of ours. I'll start painting.'

Emily moved towards the flag. Never in her life had she done anything remotely outside the law. 'Keep your nose clean,' Dad always said. 'Steer clear of them bobbies.

They'll as soon nick yo as look' – and here she was about to destroy something belonging to someone else . . . deliberately! She glanced at Louise and saw she had already finished the first long white stroke of her v. Emily tightened her hold on the flag bunting, closed the scissors and hacked. Then crouching down, she untied her bundle, selected a new flag and tied it to the pole with the four stout tapes May had sewn on. Louise had painted VOTES FOR W . . . The letters gleamed clearly in the moonlight. They would be seen for miles, Emily felt sure, if anyone was looking.

'There!' Louise finished the N with a flourish. 'Mind where you walk.'

Emily took her bundle and picked her way over the whitewash. Now she was a *law-breaker* . . . a *criminal*. She'd burned her boats . . . cut her flag! There was something oddly exciting about demonstrating her decision. The martyr part was there in the background, an unsolved dilemma, but it was too distant to worry about. What was happening now reminded her of Vic's Penny Dreadfuls. All wild adventure. Blood and thunder . . . only it was quiet as anything except for the rustle made by the two of them walking.

The next green was farther down the slope over to their left. Emily pushed through clumps of scutch grass.

'There's a great pit of sand here,' she said.

'Bunker,' Louise corrected. 'A sort of trap to catch the golf balls.'

Emily attacked her second flag, puzzling over the odd hazards of this strange game. 'What made yo pick on a golf course?'

'Private property. Owned by wealthy men, like my father. They don't like their property damaged. It's sacred. They will take a lot of notice when it's spoiled, much more than listening to reasonable argument.' There was a hardness to Louise's voice.

Her father? Was that the other reason . . . the deeper one? 'Your father will be furious.'

Louise did not answer directly, but muttered threats under her breath, one to each brushstroke. Emily caught broken phrases.

'. . . Being pig-headed . . . can't stop me . . . won't give in . . . it's my life . . . I'm not his property . . .'

So it was a twofold thing after all. One blow for Women's Rights, the other directed at her father! Which mattered most? Emily felt let down, as if this personal feud had tarnished her golden image of Louise. But perhaps the two things were connected anyway. Fathers were men and both were trouble! If anger at that final row in the kitchen had pushed her into coming, then Louise had just as much right to be forced on by her emotions. You could love and detest people at the same time, be driven to all sorts of rash acts, but it didn't mean those acts weren't *right*.

'Why did you ask *me* to come? There's all them ladies at the drawing-room meetings like Una and Maude Holiday . . . or there's Vera.'

'Ladies!' The amount of scorn Louise put into the word was remarkable. 'Meek creatures. They wouldn't say boo to a goose, let alone approve. As for Vera . . . I don't know; there's something sort of *closed*. I'd never be certain.'

'But me . . . why me?' Emily insisted.

'Because you are a fighter, like me. Nerve, courage, call it what you like. You are reliable. Besides, I like you.' She paused in mid-stroke. Emily thought she was smiling. Whitewash, dripping off her brush, made a thin white line down her skirt. 'Oh, now look what I've gone and done!'

'Here, mop it up with the matching bit on this flag.' Emily was all concern in the middle of her joy. Another link had been forged between them. Louise's pedestal, in shrinking a little, had brought friendship closer.

An owl hooted with startling clarity. Farther off came an answering call and a great white bird sailed out from a clump of skeleton trees.

'It'll be witches on broomsticks next,' Emily said shakily.

'If they do I shall rapidly paint VOTES FOR WOMEN on our remaining flags and persuade the old dears to tie them on their broomhandles. It'd be the best bit of advertising the Cause has ever had. Just think of the newspaper

The idea wasn't really funny, but they found themselves giggling on the way to the next green and the next.
Emily fumbled with the tapes, all thumbs, pulling hard,
tearing the stitching. 'Oh, blast it!'

'Tell you what, we could change over next time if you
like,' Louise offered.

'All right.'

The walking was rough. They crossed a small brook
by way of a flat wooden bridge, the noise of their footsteps shatteringly loud. Over a ridge into a second valley
and back again. Surely someone must hear? But it seemed
they had the night to themselves.

'We have to cross the farm track to the other part of
the course now,' Louise said.

They could see the farmhouse black and silver against
a quiet sky. Nine greens done, another nine and they
would be finished.

And then the dog barked. Not a single enquiring sound,
but on and on with the rattle of his chain as he ran
backwards and forwards. He knew they were there.

'It's all right, he's tied up,' Louise whispered.

'But we ain't finished.'

'We've done enough. Come on!'

They were coming out of the valley with the gate in
sight when the farmhouse door banged. A man's voice
called out:

'All right, Tiger. Down boy!' Metal chinked on stone.

'The dog's free,' Louise hissed. 'Run!' She spurted forward, Emily close on her heels. Suddenly Emily saw
Louise spread her arms, body twisting, but there was no
time to take evasive action. As Louise sprawled full length
on the turf, Emily tripped helplessly over her legs. The
remaining whitewash splashed from the can over them
both. Louise curled up, clutching her ankle. Boots crunched
over the stony track. The barking closed in.

'Go, can't you . . . run!' Louise was almost sobbing with
pain and frustration.

Emily said nothing, but moved up close to her friend,

crouching as if to shield her from attack. The dog was on them now with growls and panting breath. Too terrified to move, they waited for him to charge, but he stood, hackles raised, daring them to try.

'Sit, Tiger! And you . . . don't try anything or I'll pepper you good and proper!' The voice changed from threat to astonishment. 'Well I'll be danged . . . a couple of gels!'

But still they didn't move. Looking up, they found themselves staring into the menacing barrels of a shotgun.

7

'AND in conclusion,' the magistrate said, looking disapprovingly over the top of half-moon glasses, 'I would urge you to look carefully at your motives for such a disgraceful attack. You have behaved in an irresponsible and shameful fashion. The only mitigating circumstance would seem to be your green youth and the undoubtedly evil influence of the so-called leaders of this . . . er . . . Suffragette movement you appear to have embraced. You are fined five pounds each, with seven days to pay.'

Emily followed Louise as she limped from the dock, her heart filled with anger and despair. How would she ever find that much money in seven days? Five pounds . . . fifteen . . . fifty, were equally impossible. Would she have to go to prison instead? People did; remembering the time old Mr Nailor hit a policeman. She didn't dare look at Mam sitting pinched with shame at the back of the courtroom, or at Peter Marshall beside his frowning white-whiskered father – frosty devil! The old man had set up such a rumpus at the police station last night, treating her as if she was dirt, but she hadn't felt remorse, only burning shame at the failure. Mam was hurrying out now. Mr Marshall, grasping Louise by the elbow, was shepherding her away from the disgrace.

In her misery, Emily felt abandoned. She walked towards the door, acutely conscious of inquisitive eyes watching. Out in the corridor she heard Josiah Marshall saying:

'I shall recompense the golf club, Louise, but your fine must come out your allowance. And that is all there is to be said.' His voice was so cold and his manner so forbidding, Emily could see that for once Louise was subdued. Peter came forward to meet them and at that same moment Louise looked back at Emily. There was genuine regret in her expression. She mouthed: 'I'm sorry!' and turned to her brother. An almost imperceptible understanding passed between them. Emily saw him incline his head as Josiah propelled her away. Peter didn't go with them, but instead came towards her.

'I am very sorry about all this. Louise and I would like to help, but we don't wish to cause you embarrassment.'

Emily hesitated, not knowing what to say.

'Please accept this as a gift from friends.' He quietly and firmly pressed a folded note into her hand.

She took it, mumbling: 'Thank yo . . . thank yo!' not wanting to look directly at him because of embarrassment.

'You don't want to take Louise too seriously,' he said, touching her arm. 'She means well, but she's too impetuous as a rule, and ends up in the most awful scrapes. You might get hurt.' He smiled briefly and walked away.

Perplexed by his words and dazzled by his generosity which left her with uneasy feelings of shame, she went to look for her mother. Together they walked home in silence, worse than any amount of Mam's usual scolding. The streets looked grey and grim under a leaden sky and the thin drizzle was in tune with her swirling muddled thoughts. Bitterness was uppermost and shame too, but a tiny living germ of rebellion persisted in jumping into the forefront of her mind.

That magistrate with his well-cut suit and fish eyes, what did he know about being a woman? He just sat there doling out punishments – authority as familiar as his own watch-chain. Just see how he'd feel after a month or so peeling spuds, raking out the ashes, washing and ironing, bending over a sewing machine. The seams would be crooked, that's for sure! And not a thread of power to hang around him!

The kettle was simmering at the side of the range when they got home. Mam opened the hot-plate, pushed the kettle over the flames, then fetched the ironstone teapot and a couple of mugs.

Emily hesitated, not taking off her coat. 'I'd best be getting back to work, Mam.'

'Have a cup of tea before yo goes.' Mam did not look at her. There seemed an invisible barrier between them.

Emily wanted desperately to explain how she felt, but words, as always, eluded her.

'I don't want yo to worry,' was all she could say.

Mashing the tea, Mam made a sound between a snort and a sob. 'Life's a bugger,' she said suddenly. 'Luck don't come into it much. If there's anything to be got, yo has to grab it where you can.'

Emily could hardly believe her ears. She had expected a tirade. 'Yo ain't angry then?'

For the first time, Mam looked at her, a shadow of a smile creasing her worn face. She pushed away a wisp of grey hair. 'Yo don't know nothing,' she said. 'I've spent my life battling to keep things agoing. God knows I've tried, but now . . .' she shrugged. 'I'm tired. Yo're a woman now; seventeen. I can't shelter yo for ever. If yo wants to strike out on your own I'm not stopping yo.' She leaned forward across the table, pushing a mug of tea towards Emily. 'But I'll not have yo dragging this family through the mud. Make your protest somewhere else if yo ain't satisfied with your station. As for that fine . . . there's two pound under the clock. Yo can take your Grandma's wedding ring, that pair of linen sheets and your bicycle round to Mr Isaac's. We've been good customers, he'll likely pawn them for the other three quid. Yo can have five bob out of your wages each week till it's paid off.'

Emily was choked with tears. This totally unexpected aid had caught her off guard. Anger would have been easier to deal with.

'There's no need,' she muttered. 'Peter Marshall gave me the money.'

Mam stared at her. 'And yo took it?' She was angry but half relieved.

'Yes.'

'So there is something between yo . . . seems your Dad was right after all. Yo'd better be careful. A gent like him don't take notice of a girl of your class for any honest reason.'

'Oh, don't be ridiculous!' Responding to the anger dried her tears. 'I ain't nothing to him. It was just kindness.

75

Don't think I'd have taken it if there'd been a choice. I'm not daft.' Emily gulped her red-hot tea, burning her mouth. The barrier was back, but she knew there had been sympathy. For a brief second she'd been privileged to see the woman who lived inside the body of Mam. It wasn't the first time Emily had wondered about her mother as an individual, but it was the first time she had experienced her. It left her curiously humbled.

'I'll be off then.'

Mam got up and began collecting the mugs. As Emily opened the back door she said: 'Tread careful. With a bit of luck Mrs Harris'll overlook all this.'

But she was wrong.

'In here, Miss Palmer.' Mrs Harris, her face set in lines of disapproval, beckoned from the door of the fitting-room.

A tense hush stretched over the workroom, broken only by the rustle of cloth and Flo's nervous giggle. Emily crossed to the fitting-room, went inside and closed the door. Mrs Harris was standing by a brightly burning fire which did nothing towards melting the ice of the atmosphere. She took a packet from the mantelpiece, opened it and counted out the coins.

'Nine shillings and sixpence. A full week's wages although it is only Monday. As you've not had the agreed week's notice, I'm paying you for the whole week instead. But you needn't come to me for a reference.'

Injustice burned worse than her sore mouth. The whole day had been an insult. And now this!

'But why?'

Mrs Harris looked at her as if she were simple. 'Had up in court this morning and you ask why?'

Oh for Louise's silver tongue! But she wasn't going to leave without saying anything.

'Don't yo care about how things are for us?' she burst out. That floored her! Ma Harris was gaping like a fish out of water. 'Us women I mean. We've no rights.'

'You've the right to work hard and mind your manners, miss!' Ma Harris had recovered before Emily had time to form any more arguments. 'Take your money and collect your belongings. There's no need to work out the day.'

The niggling frustrations which had been there for as long as Emily could remember, and which had budded into recognizable shape under Louise's influence, spiked into a great cactus flower of anger which demolished any hope of words, but had to be expressed. Emily marched to the door, opened it and stood in the doorway in full view of her workmates, then slowly and deliberately made the rudest gesture she knew, just as she had done to Willie Green the Sunday of her first bicycle ride. With a feeling of triumph which splintered into fragments even before she had finished closing the door, Emily went to collect the scissors and thimble which were all that belonged to her. She'd regret the money later, but for now she could no more have taken it than fly over the moon. One bite of charitable cake was enough in a single day.

No one dared talk, but there were irrepressible snuffles of laughter.

Alice whispered: 'Good gel!' but there were no other offers of encouragement. Only from Vera did she receive a long strange look. Emily felt as if she were being offered a mysterious present she could not identify. Another time she might have responded; today she walked from the room, down the stairs and out into the street.

Two weeks later Emily answered a knock at the back door and found Vera standing there.

'You was splendid, Emmie. Mad but splendid!' Hugging her, Vera coughed in the sharp air.

Emily was so amazed she almost forgot to draw her inside.

'I'd have come round that same night only I felt bad and went back to me lodgings and bed. Been there ever since.' She coughed again.

'Here, come inside,' Emily said. 'Yo sound as if yo didn't ought to have got up.'

'Oh, I'm all right.' Vera was brimming with suppressed excitement. 'I've news for you.' Two spots of feverish colour burned on her cheeks. 'I've left Ma Harris's. Got a job in London. Look, I had this letter from Mrs Silver

– I used to know her before. She came to the house where I was in service, to do plain sewing. She's set up in business now for herself; got premises in Soho and she's done that well she needs help. So she wrote and asked me, as we've always kept in touch.'

'I'm ever so pleased for yo,' Emily said, bowled over by the surprise. Vera in service in London! She felt again the growing affection for her which had first developed from the comradeship of the bicycle parade. The extraordinary hug and the sharing of news took her breath away.

'There's something else an' all,' Vera added. 'Mrs Silver wants two girls. Asked me if I knew anyone. Of course I thought of you.'

If Emily had been astonished before, she was completely dumbfounded now. Vera burst into unaccustomed laughter which changed into a fit of coughing, bringing Emily out of her stupor.

'Come by the fire. There's a pot of tea on the hob. Yo have a drink and get your breath. I was just getting some tea for May. She'll be back from school in a jiffy.' She poured a mug of tea and gave it to Vera. 'I never knew yo had worked in London.'

For once Vera was willing to talk about herself. 'Lived near Hyde Park. A tall house with iron railings round – in one of them London squares with a garden and trees in the middle and a mews at the back where horses and carriages were kept.'

'Sounds very grand,' Emily said, knowing nothing of London, but wanting to keep the suggestion of confidences going.

'It was right enough.'

Emily moved a little farther out along the tightrope. 'Tweeny were yo?'

'Parlourmaid,' Vera corrected her. A note of bitterness crept into her voice. 'I would have been cook . . . that's what I intended.'

'What happened?' As soon as she asked, Emily knew the confidences were over. The old tight look had returned and Vera merely shrugged her shoulders, burying her nose in the mug of tea. Mam's arrival with a bundle of washing prevented the live tension from growing.

'Yo're off work early, Vera,' she said. 'My word, it's cold! There'll be some sleet before long. It's a good thing there ain't such a load today.'

'Mam's found herself a little job,' Emily explained. 'Washes for three or four folks round the Vicarage. I help with a bit of ironing.' She poured some tea. 'Take the weight off your feet, Mam, I've got a surprise for yo.'

'What's that then?' Mam pulled off her shoes and pushed her feet near the range.

'I've an offer of a job.'

Mam set her mug down on the table carefully, then she sniffed and rubbed the back of her hand across her nose. 'Doing what?' she asked.

'To go to London with Vera and work for a lady that runs a dressmaking business there.'

'In London?' The obvious relief was tempered with doubt. 'That's a long way off.'

'What's a long way off?' May asked, limping into the kitchen, her face sharpened with cold.

'London,' Emily said. 'I'm going to work there.'

'Oh, Emmie, yo ain't?' May looked at her with such distress Emily was torn apart. She almost decided there and then not to go, but knew she couldn't stay on at home like this. No one round about was willing to take her on after the trouble with the police, and the thought of London had an edgy attraction. There were the Suffragettes too, marching and demonstrating. Hardly a week passed without news of windows shattered, houses gutted by fire, letter-boxes attacked with acid. She could be part of all that, bravely, without hanging on to Louise's apron strings. There would be no family to involve. Standing alone like Joan of Arc, without the stake. But she'd face other things, prison, hunger strikes, even forcible feeding . . .

The glow of this heroic daydream was shattered by May bursting into tears. Emily went and put her arms round her, hugging her tight, all the excitement collapsing into a tired heap. But there was still fact.

'Don't cry, my lovie. We won't be parted for ever. I'll be back to see yo. Or yo can come for a visit.' She was making it up as she went along without real thought except to try and stop these sobs that were like knives stabbing at her.

'Give over, May,' Mam said with less sympathy. 'Here, sit down and get your tea. A bit of food inside yo'll put a different face on things. Our Emmie can't hang round this house for ever without work.'

The back door opened and Vic came in with a gust of freezing air, slinging his cap on the table. 'What's this then, somebody died?' He saw Vera and stopped, colour flooding his face. The surprise trapped his emotions for anyone to see and Emily buried her face in May's thick hair, feeling like a peeping Tom.

'Our Emmie's off to London with Vera,' Mam said brutally. 'They're going to work for someone Vera knows . . . sewing.'

He looked from Vera to Emily and said in a low voice: 'That right?'

There was nothing to say except 'Yes', pleasure and excitement stone dead. A taut silence stretched over the kitchen, disturbed only by May's snivels.

'When will yo be off?' Vic asked at last.

'Soon as we can.' Vera tried to speak as if nothing was out of joint. 'In a few days I should think. After I've sent a message to let Mrs Silver know we're coming.'

The quietness clamped down again. Emily felt in the pocket of her apron and found a handkerchief. She began mopping at May's cheeks, then helped her to sit down. Cutting the loaf on the table with unsteady strokes, busying herself pouring tea, she felt the tense atmosphere in the stuffy kitchen screw tighter and tighter. If the loud knock on the door had not happened, Emily was sure she would have picked up one of the mugs and hurled it on the floor. As it was they looked at one another; startled. A knock on the *front* door? No one came that way except on special occasions. Weddings, funerals . . . disaster!

Emily took off her apron, patting her hair. 'I'll go.' She went into the parlour, firmly closing the dividing door.

Whoever it was, she would rather not have a listening audience. She was even more relieved she had shut it when she saw Peter Marshall standing on the pavement. The Maudslay was outside and there were enough popping eyes and noses squashed against windows to fill the church hall!

'Please won't yo come in?' Emily said hastily.

Peter smiled, taking off his smart touring cap as he came into the room. He was good-looking, there was no denying. Tall. And he smelled nice. Pears soap and tweed cloth sweetened by fresh air. Emily was flustered by his bold confidence and steady gaze, very conscious of the difference between the rich comforts of the Tower House and the shabby threadbare room in which they stood. She wished Ernie wouldn't insist on laying his Sunday trousers along the top of the sideboard with the braces dangling. Peter seemed unconcerned. After one glance round which seared her pride, he produced a pale lilac envelope from his pocket and held it out.

'Lou asked me to bring this. 'Fraid it's the first opportunity I've had. Since the . . . er . . . golf course business Father has been keeping a tight rein. Lou is confined to the house and I am being pressed to join the delights of business management.' He pulled such a wry face that Emily couldn't suppress a giggle. She took the envelope. There was so little time. In a moment he would be gone and that mustn't happen without a word of thanks. The whole affair was galling, but he had saved her from a tight corner, possibly prison. Saved pawning her bicycle, too. She scrambled after her vanishing wits.

'I'm that grateful,' she said baldly. He raised enquiring eyebrows. 'For getting me out of that mess. I can't pay yo back at present. Things have been a bit . . . tight. Money I mean. But when I start my new job in London I'll send the money regular. Yo won't mind if it's in small amounts? I don't suppose I shall be able to manage more than two and a tanner a week.' She was guessing wildly. Vera had said nothing about how much they would earn, and there would be board and lodging to pay. Goodness knows what other expenses.

D

Peter looked embarrassed, which surprised her and brought him on more of a level. 'Don't think about it. Regard the fine as my contribution to Women's Rights.' Was he mocking? If he was it was in a gentle way. His expression held open friendliness.

'But I can't accept . . .' she began.

'Rubbish!' he said. 'I don't want to hear another word on the subject.'

'But won't your father be angry?'

Peter laughed. A great resounding bell of laughter. 'I don't tell him about things like that.'

Fancy having five pounds to hand out as you pleased! The gap between them pulled further apart. She stood clutching the letter, not knowing what to say or do.

He turned towards the door, hesitated and turned back again. 'What was that about going to London?'

'Vera Bradshaw and me. We've been offered places working for a dressmaker she knows in Soho, that's part of London.' It was like talking about the moon, it was so outside her experience.

'When do you start?' Peter asked.

'I don't know yet. Vera's only just told me. Why?'

'I was just thinking . . . perhaps not . . .' He frowned, juggling with an idea. Then he smiled. 'It wouldn't half be a lark.'

'What?'

He rubbed his hands together, grinning at her. 'I ought to explain that Louise and I are travelling to London next week. It's a face-saver for Father, you see. Ever since Lou was in court he's felt that all his friends and business associates were looking a bit sideways at him. The odd sly digs and that sort of thing. So he decided Easter should be spent with Aunt Gertrude and Uncle Henry.' He turned the names into a ponderous weighty meal. Emily felt herself smiling. 'Father will travel up by train later, business being what it is. A nice long holiday is his remedy for wagging tongues, and under Aunt Gertrude's strict regime Lou won't be able to call her soul her own, let alone join in any more Suffragette pranks.' He glanced at her sharply, surprising the antagonism before she could disguise it. 'Oh, don't be too hard on him. He's got old-fashioned ideas about women. But what I was going to suggest is giving you a seat in the car. Miss Bradshaw too, if she wishes. There's plenty of room for four and all the luggage. Most of Lou's is going by goods train. She's rather keen on her wardrobe! What do you say?'

Thoughts flew about in her head like little birds, eluding capture. She'd save on money. No train fare. Dad would slaughter her. Mam too. But the bicycle, she wouldn't have to sell it to raise cash. And what fun. She was as nervous as anything. They'd need hot water-bottles if they weren't to freeze to death in this weather, and didn't you have to wear special motoring hats – yards of tulle to tie under your chin?

'Well?'

She *had* to say something. 'Thanks ever so!'

'I *am* glad!' he said, and catching hold of her hand pumped it up and down. 'Wednesday then. We'll call round for you nice and early. Say half past nine.'

'Oh no!' She sounded so appalled that he stopped pumping but kept hold of her hand.

'What's wrong?'

'I . . . er . . . we'd better meet yo somewhere else . . . er . . . down by the corner of Summer Hill Terrace and Sandpits. Easier for Vera. She won't have to carry her bag so far.' It was a lie, but she simply couldn't have him calling round for her. It would be enough to make Dad stay away from work and start a fight. She must get rid of him. There were shuffling noises coming from the kitchen. Any moment now, Mam would be in here. 'Half past nine then, at Sandpits.' What a fateful place to choose! Was it a pointer of things to come? Destiny? She wriggled her hand free and went to open the door.

'Au revoir,' Peter said. 'I'll tell Lou. Don't crumple the letter before you've read it!' He got into the car.

Emily closed the door before he had started the engine. Her heart was pounding and her cheeks ready to go up in flames. She leaned back for support, feeling the hard wood against her spine. The letter *was* crushed. She smoothed the paper. Things had a way of repeating themselves.

First the accident and now this fresh meeting, both at the turn into Sandpits. Exchanges of paper between herself and Peter. But there was no time for reading now, even if Louise's bold script wasn't dancing about. Emily slipped the envelope into the pocket of her skirt, put her hands to her burning cheeks in a vain effort to cool them, then, with a deep breath, braced herself for all the questions to come.

8

EMILY was making pictures from the ragged clouds in an effort to keep thoughts of the journey to London on the rim of her mind. Giant faces with grinning mouths and ears like saucers, monstrous birds drifted and merged into a ship with billowing sails.

'I hate hanging about,' Vera said, blowing her nose which was red with cold. 'I'm starved already. D'you think we'll get there without turning into ice? We ought to have gone by train.'

'And spend all that money we ain't got,' Emily retorted with a confidence she was far from feeling. For two pins she'd pack up her basket and the old cardboard box, and run back up Summer Hill Terrace.

The church clock began ringing out the half hour.

'They're late,' Vera said.

'Hardly!' At least she wasn't alone in feeling nervous. She glanced up the hill almost expecting to see Dad on the coal cart. She'd never know how she'd got away without Mam coming to see her off. All those tears . . . May had shed buckets. Why did nothing ever work out entirely happy? There was always some snag. Leaving May was the only thing she truly regretted. That and Vic's silent misery at being parted from Vera. But the letter from Louise was heartwarming. The things she'd written . . . about being ashamed to have got her into so much trouble . . . and all that about having formed a deep and lasting friendship based firmly in their shared misfortune and shared future as Women . . . and finally, her regret at being forcibly parted.

Thinking about it made her shiver, but not with cold. Louise would never have written at all if she'd known they were to go to London together! She was glad things had worked out this way.

There they were! Louise waving from the front seat

of the Maudslay, which had a large leather travelling trunk strapped on the roof. She pushed aside the tartan rug as the car halted and climbed down on to the pavement.

'You don't know how pleased I am to see you both,' she said. 'The last three weeks have been dreadful. Father has been most unco-operative and I've felt like a prisoner, stuck in the house. But maybe it's been good training!'

She was as defiant as ever, and as boisterous. Emily still had the feeling that everything to Louise was a game, in spite of the sincerity of her letter.

'I'm coming in the back with you two,' Louise went on. 'Then we can have a good old gossip and swop news.'

Emily glanced at Peter who had got out and was stowing the luggage beside the driving seat. All he said was: 'I hope you'll be comfortable,' looking at her rather longer than necessary which set her heart thumping.

'There are hot bottles under the rugs,' Louise said as they got in, 'and we've brought food and brandy in case we get perished, though we can always stop and buy some hot tea on the way.'

Emily was relieved by all this preparation. Perhaps travelling would be less hazardous than she had feared. A whole new life, she was thinking as the streets slid by. Trams, carts, horses, people, shops, factories and railways smoking, cobblestones, church towers and chimney-stacks. The great dingy glorious awful mass that was her Brum, slipping behind as the streets tidied into neat roads with larger houses and then became lanes twisting through meadows and brown furrowed fields. She didn't want to go back, but a piece of her life was being chopped away and she was choked.

But the journey turned out a joy. It was a diamond of a day, sharp and sparkling with sunshine and the pleasure of flowering friendship. Even the country wasn't so bad, Emily decided, though it made her vaguely uncomfortable. It was so wide open! They talked almost non-stop, Louise getting more and more intense about all she hoped to do for the Cause, showing them the newspapers *Votes for Women* and *Suffragette*, explaining about the split in the

Women's Social and Political Union, with Mrs Pankhurst and Christabel emerging triumphant as leaders and the Pethick Lawrences retiring into the background as editors of the quieter newspaper *Votes for Women*. Even with the picnic break, by the time they reached the outskirts of London in the late afternoon, Emily's head was buzzing and Vera looked unusually flushed.

'I've no intention of staying cooped up in Aunt Gertrude's great house like I was at home,' Louise continued. 'She may be strict, but there are ways of slipping through *her* fingers. Just in case there are problems in that direction I have a plan all worked out.'

It involves me, Emily thought, enchanted and alarmed.

'Such a piece of luck, you coming to London, *and* to do sewing. I couldn't have arranged it better. I shall see that Aunt Gertrude makes use of your talents, either as personal dressmaker or for plain sewing. And I shall need some more dresses. If I'm to stay in London over Easter there are bound to be plenty of social occasions. If I'm involved with women's fripperies it will put Father's mind at rest. So you see we have a perfect grapevine; tailor made!' and she laughed in a way that made them both join in.

'I'm a sort of go-between?' Emily asked.

'That's right. Vera too.'

'I'm not sure,' Vera said, sounding doubtful. 'We aren't working for ourselves, Miss Marshall.'

'I know that, but I'm prepared to be a genuine customer. And please don't call me Miss Marshall all the time. If we're to be comrades in arms there simply mustn't be such formality.'

Emily picked up the *Suffragette* which had slithered from Louise's knee on to the floor. Holding the paper in her hand, she experienced a strong feeling of the reality it represented. The reports it contained of wild defiant acts committed by women all over England, made decorating the golf greens seem truly part of a whole movement. She could not work out in detail why this should be, too tired by now to sort her thoughts. She looked out of the window at the shops and houses and hurrying people. It was different from Birmingham and yet both cities had something in common – a rush and noise that put her at ease and made her feel at home.

It was in a broad street filled with the clatter of drays and the whining clang of trams that the car began to lurch and bump, jolting them like rag dolls. Peter pulled into the kerb.

'Now what?' Louise said, and got out.

It was a puncture, Emily saw as she followed her. One of the front tyres was as flat as a pancake.

'It could have been worse,' Peter said. 'We've done pretty well to get this far without mishaps. I'll have to change the wheel.'

Vera and Emily looked at each other.

'It shouldn't take long,' Peter said, guessing their thoughts. 'About a quarter of an hour. I've everything to hand, tools, spare wheel . . .'

For once he was wrong. The wheel change went smoothly enough, but the car, having stopped, had a fit of temperament and refused to start once more, despite Peter's most dextrous coaxing.

Shops were closing and people beginning the homeward trek. The stuffy warmth in the car had disappeared with the opening of doors and Vera shivered.

'Perhaps we ought to make our own way,' she said to Louise. 'We could take the underground train, there's a station farther along the street. If we go to Oxford Circus it's only a short walk after that.'

'Very well,' Louise said. 'But write your address for me before you go. We can't come this far, then lose track of each other.' She leaned out of the window. 'Did you hear, Pete? They are going by train.'

It was a strangely harassed Peter who came up from the depths of the engine. 'Sensible idea. We'll have to get a tow. Lord knows what time we'll get to Holland Park. Aunt Gertrude will have alerted the police and started dragging the Thames by then!' He grinned with returning good humour. 'Sorry I can't help you down with your luggage.' He held out hands black with oil and grease.

'It don't matter,' Emily said and found the nerve to

add: 'We should help ourselves, remember?'

He smiled more broadly. 'I *do* hope we'll meet again soon. I'll be here for some time, with a bit of luck.'

'For the ballooning,' Louise added. 'He's mad keen to join the Aero Club at Hurlingham. You can imagine what Father has to say about that! It's only one step up from Suffragetting, as far as he's concerned.'

Following Vera into the depths of the underground station after exchanging addresses and goodbyes, Emily had no thoughts to spare for anything but the terrifying claustrophobic passages and steps that wound on and down swallowing them up, and when they reached the platform, having juggled with their belongings and clutched their hats which were being grabbed by the warm persistent wind, she was quite exhausted.

'It is a bit queer the first time you come into one of these places,' Vera said, as they sat down on a wooden bench. 'But you get used to it.'

I never will, Emily thought – hearing a hollow eerie roar which reached a crescendo as the train shot from the tunnel with an explosion of sound – this is my first and last time! Inside the compartment, reassured by Vera's calm and the way other passengers treated the experience with no more concern than they would washing the backs of their necks or drinking a cup of tea, other thoughts came creeping back into Emily's mind. She was still quaking inside and more than relieved to get out and emerge like a mole into the daylight of Oxford Circus, but there was room to wonder what Mrs Silver would be like, whether she would be a tyrant or fidgety like Ma Harris or even if she would employ them for long. Vera's descriptions left a lot to the imagination.

Wide streets were left behind as they wormed farther into the heart of Soho. Buildings hunched above them, reducing the fading daylight even more. The way was cluttered with barrows of fruit, delivery drays, cabs and people. Mouth-watering smells drifted from the little shops and cafés they passed – coffee, garlic, roasting cheese.

'I could eat a horse,' Emily said.

'But you won't.' Vera gave one of her rare smiles. 'Ten

to one Mrs Silver will have a supper of meat balls in the best gravy you've ever tasted.'

In a small street beyond a French baker's and a wholesale tweed merchant's, Vera stopped outside a brown-painted door with a fanlight. Narrow stone steps led down to a dingy area above which a shop window with squared panes eyed them.

B. SILVER — COURT DRESSMAKER — Emily read the lettering on the shop sign and as Vera tapped on the door, felt suddenly very nervous indeed.

The door was opened by a dumpy woman who had a rather large head. She was dressed plainly in unrelieved black, a colour which was taken up by her thick eyebrows and tightly coiled hair. Only a few bold strands dared to make lines of white. With her hooked nose and dark probing eyes she looked all the things Emily had feared. But the delectable smell that crept out around her was encouraging and so was her lop-sided smile, which entirely broke up the stern expression changing frown lines into smile creases. It was a transformation.

'Vera, my dear, it's a treat to see you . . . and Emily. I may call you Emily? Miss Palmer seems so formal, with Vera being such an old friend.' Mrs Silver's London accent was a foreign sound to Emily. She caught a hand of each girl and her grip was strong and dry. 'Come in . . . come in!'

The bustle that followed, Emily was to learn, was typical of her new employer. She moved at a trot, whisking through work and leisure with equal speed. Even her habit of reading the daily newspaper, in time to sit down at the breakfast table precisely at seven-thirty, was done in record time, and never a word missed.

Now, in the narrow hall, papered in rumbustious dark-red roses, Emily hardly had time to take in the aspidistra standing on a bamboo table, in fact she missed it by inches as they were swept up two flights of creaking stairs to an attic bedroom with a sloping roof and dormer windows, which she and Vera were to share. It was sparsely furnished, but immaculately clean. Bunches of red cherries glowed down from the wallpaper on to white honeycomb bedspreads; bright rag rugs were set by each bed and in front of the washstand; a curtained alcove was supplied with hooks for their hanging clothes, the rest would go into a large chest of drawers.

'Supper in ten minutes,' Mrs Silver said, hand on the doorknob ready to take flight. 'Meat balls today. A favourite with you I know, Vera.'

'What did I tell you?' Vera said when she had gone downstairs.

Emily flopped on to the bed in a whirl.

'Better look sharp,' Vera added. 'She was always a stickler for time. Ten minutes means nine.'

Unpacking would have to wait, Emily decided, though she'd dearly love to strip down to the waist and have a really good wash and put on a fresh blouse. A lick and a promise would have to do, with a comb through her hair.

Supper, which they ate in a cheerful kitchen under the watchful eye of an elderly parrot in a wicker cage, was delicious. Meat balls with plenty of creamed potatoes and nutty carrots. Afterwards a marvellous concoction which Mrs Silver called 'Apple Strudel' – adding: 'Something special for a special day, so help yourself to cream. It won't be like this every day, though I keep a good table. Nothing like good food to produce good work.' She gave Emily a second helping. 'It's real nice to have company for meals. Since Brenda left I've been on my own . . . tedious eating like that.'

'Brenda worked for yo?' Emily asked.

'Been with me two years. Very good worker. She left to get married. I wanted to keep her on, but her young man said no.' She shrugged. 'Course, I have other workers. Miss Feather comes in each day and there's one or two do specialities for me at home, button-holing, things like that. You'll meet them all tomorrow. After supper I'll show you the workroom.'

It was in the basement and stretched from the front to the back of the house. Daylight obviously meant little, but there was a plentiful supply of gas-mantles. To Emily's experienced eye the table space was generous, one each if her calculations were right, with three treadle sewing machines and a long cutting table stretching the width of the room under the barred area window. Whitewash lightened the rough brick walls against which were rows of shelving stacked with bolts of cloth and work in various stages of completion, and a vast chest of large and small drawers crammed with bobbins, patterns, hooks and eyes, whalebone, needles, pins and every conceivable need.

One thing was sure, Mrs Silver must be doing a steady trade to be so well stocked. It made the future more rosy, Emily was thinking as she smiled and nodded and answered the questions fired at her about her life and family and sewing experience, surprisingly in that order.

When they were finally alone in their bedroom, Emily let out a great gasp. 'I feel like something left over after a whirlwind's passed by,' she said to Vera. 'Is she always like this?'

Vera stepped out of her brown dress, slipped it on to a hanger and straightened cuffs and collar before replying: 'She was always on the go. The only thing that slows her down is one of her attacks of lumbago.'

'On the go! That's a mild way to put it.' Emily eased off her best boots and flexed her toes. 'But I like her . . . so long as she don't expect me to sew fast as the wind!'

In bed, when the candle was snuffed and the street-lamps made goblins out of the room shadows, Emily lay for some time with her eyes wide open, worn out but unable to sleep. With the sound of Vera's sleep-breathing, she slipped out of bed, wrapped the quilt round her shoulders and went to look out of the dormer window into the strange narrow street. A cat was stalking along the pavement and two lovers passed, arms entwined. Vera began to snore, then once or twice coughed in restless sleep.

And what of Louise and Peter? Emily looked across at the opposite rooftop and saw an upturned moon sitting on a chimneypot. Would they all meet again? There was an awful gap to part them, for all that Louise might say. Leisure and work. Money and no money. Birth! Yes, it was a yawning gap all right. Loneliness touched her.

Well, she had Vera didn't she? Even if May and Vic and the rest of them were miles away. She looked round at the shallow mound in the bed, just visible, and was swamped by a feeling of total isolation. It was so powerful, she could do nothing but stand there struggling to bear it.

'Yo great daft lump!' The sound of her own voice dispelled the loneliness enough to allow her to climb back into bed and burrow under the bedclothes.

9

EMILY paused on her way back to Mrs Silver's to buy one of the weekly news-sheets from a young woman who looked as if she would be more at home in a drawing-room than on the kerb. Handing over a ha'penny, she tucked her parcel of bugle beads and silver thread under her arm and began avidly reading Suffragette news. In the April weeks that passed over Easter and stretched into May and then June, Emily had found herself increasingly involved, though with discretion. The police were hunting the leaders and Parliament had passed a new bill that was sheer torture. Prisoners on hunger strike were freed before their sentences were complete, only to be re-arrested once health returned. With these new pressures, the movement had gone underground, but was just as active. Every week newspaper headlines cried: GIGANTIC FIRE – BOMB EX-PLOSION – MORE LETTER BOX ATTACKS – GOLF GREENS CUT UP – MANSION FIRED – WINDOWS SMASHED.

In spite of Mrs Silver's clock-watching ways, Emily had managed to attend several of the Hyde Park meetings. What 'larks' (as Louise put it) went on! Successions of speakers popping up out of the crowd. The police could never win. As they arrested one, another would jump on a stool and carry on speaking. Louise had done it, spur of the moment, on one of the jaunts when she outwitted Aunt Gertrude. The crowd for the most part had matched the good-nature and repartee of the women, but Emily had observed the rough handling some speakers received and sensed a real enmity. It was no game after all.

'Git back to yer 'usband and kids,' shouted one heckler. 'If yer don't we'll give yer something to remember.'

For months they had been harassed by nameless hooligans who materialized whenever there was trouble with the police. As she folded the news-sheet and began making her way past Liberty's, Emily thought cynically that it was the way of the world – bullies lying in wait for the chance to torment anyone weaker than themselves. Well, they'd show them women were tough. There had been enough demonstrations of that already – hunger strikes, beatings taken, and still they came back for more. Emily flexed her muscles, grateful for once for their stocky power. She might not be one of those fragile beauties in *Home Notes*, but she could pack a useful punch if need be.

'Oh there you are, Emily. What took you so long, my dear? Did you get everything?' Mrs Silver turned from the tailor's dummy swathed in yellow satin, looking over steel-rimmed glasses.

'Everything except the cording.' Emily took off her coat and hat, hanging them on the stand behind the door. She breathed in the sweet warm smell of the flat irons. 'Mr Bootley said he can order, so I told him to do that. It'll take five days though.'

Mrs Silver shook her head, tutting over the slipshod ways of other establishments. She was a stickler for prompt service and good workmanship, as Emily had found to her cost when forgetting to trim a ragged seam and whip it correctly.

'Attend to detail, Emily, and the whole will take care of itself,' Mrs Silver had said, and then made her work overtime to finish the garment. She eased her back now, saying: 'This wretched lumbago's plaguing me today. I'll have to take a dose and see if I can't shift it.' She went out of the workroom and stiffly up the stairs.

'There's a letter for you,' Vera murmured as Emily sat down and began threading a needle. She pushed it across the table.

May's careful copperplate!

Emily found it suddenly difficult to see the needle's eye. She blinked fiercely. No time for reading now. The letter would have to wait. She stowed it in her skirt pocket.

'I got a news-sheet,' she whispered to Vera. 'Mrs Pankhurst's been released from Holloway again. They'll surely not re-arrest her after the trouble last time.'

'Course they will.' Vera bit through her silk twist with a viciousness that betrayed her feelings. 'Wicked, letting her out just to get well after starving, only to whisk her back. Cat and Mouse is just the right nickname for that ... Law!'

Emily glanced at her. Vera never swore, but could make an ordinary word into an obscenity if her feelings ran high. She looked stirred, face flushed and breathing harsh.

'Yo all right?' Emily asked.

'Good enough.'

They sewed in silence for a while. On the opposite side of the room Miss Feather, grey and wispy, was sniffing monotonously over the bodice she was embroidering. Vera's scissors clipped at a seam and from over their heads came the sound of Mrs Silver plodding about the kitchen. The subdued work-sounds irritated Emily. Not that she disliked her job, there was interest even with the long hours, but a frustration had been building in her over the weeks. More and more she wanted time to be active for the Cause.

'I've popped the kettle on while I was up there,' Mrs Silver said, closing the door behind her. 'Nothing to beat a good strong cup of tea . . . better than all your medicine. Nip up in a couple of minutes, Emily, and make us all a cup.'

Emily finished the hem she was turning and left the workroom, glad of the opportunity to read May's letter. The kettle was singing and she poured water into the teapot, then began reading while she waited for it to mash.

It seems ever so long since you went, I don't like sleeping by myself as I get the shivers. Things are bad here. Mrs Harris says she won't have no more Palmers and I can't find work nowhere else. So couldn't I come and work with you? I am neat at sewing, you can tell Mrs Silver and it would help Mam and Dad as Mam will soon not be able to bend with the new baby coming nor help me so much and Dad is out of work because Mrs Barnet has sold the business since her husband died. Vic says to give his respects to Vera. He is on strike and says he is fed up and wants to go for a soldier. If he does I can't bear it with just Ernie and Mam all scratchy, so can't I come? I miss you something awful.

Your loving sister,
May xxxxx

Emily pushed the letter back in her pocket and poured the tea with a shaking hand. Oh God, Mam expecting and Dad off work. Poor little mite, it was a cry from the heart. What were those two fools at, saddling themselves with another snivelling brat. Mam must be the wrong end of forty if she was a day. Emily put the sugar bowl on the tray with the cups and took them back into the workroom. She slopped the tea handing it to Mrs Silver, who looked at her shrewdly.

'Something bothering you, Emily?'

Now for it. Nothing like asking. Silly to feel nervous — after all she was as different again from old Ma Harris.

'It's my sister. She wants to come and work for yo,' Emily blurted out. Why couldn't she say things sweet, instead of slapping the words down, take it or leave it, like so much wet fish? 'She's that miserable and can't rightly do for herself like I told yo, because she's lame. But she's a dab hand with a needle and willing. I'd look after her, just board and keep that's all. She could have part of my wages for her own bits.' The words were pouring out now, but not smooth and silken, more like a rough piece of sacking. There was a look of doubt on Mrs Silver's face. As a last desperate measure, Emily pushed the letter at her, closed her eyes and prayed.

'Drink your tea, my dear. We'll discuss this later,' Mrs Silver said.

It was over an hour before anything more was said. When Mrs Silver spoke it was casually, after presenting Emily with a large box to deliver to Mrs Henry Boston of Holland Park.

'Take this, my dear. You know the address. Quick as you can. I'll advance you the omnibus fare . . . oh and about your sister. I could do with more help. How old is she?'

'Twelve last March.'

Mrs Silver's eyebrows arched. 'Twelve! I thought . . . no matter. I'll take her anyway. There's a lot to be said for training someone in your own methods. Tell her to get here as soon as she can.'

Emily was so bursting with a quantity of feelings she seized Mrs Silver's hand in both of hers and kissed it. She couldn't speak at all. Just as quickly she dropped the hand and, with burning cheeks, picked up the box and rushed out into the street.

'Well I never did!' Mrs Silver patted her hair and adjusted her dress, putting her disturbed feelings back into position.

Emily's heart was singing all the way to Holland Park. She smiled at the conductor, at the people in the bus, in the street, coming out of shops, and stopped to buy a bunch of violets from an old woman with a flower basket.

The stately Holland Park house frowned on such good spirits, but Emily didn't care. It was the sort of day when everything went right, so Louise was bound to be in and with even more luck, Aunt Gertrude Boston might be out.

The day did not fail. Emily found herself ushered into a chintz-covered sitting-room which looked out on to an old walled garden full of tumbling rhododendrons. The room was as untidy as the fallen magenta petals outside, with a scattering of books and newspapers. Gloves and coat had been draped over a chair and an extravagant hat left on a small table beneath an oval mirror. Louise was there, as lovely as ever in a flowered tea-gown, the afternoon sun picking colours from her hair. She got up from the couch where she had been sitting beside a small dark woman in a restrained green suit.

'Emily Palmer! Where have you been all these weeks?' Louise put her hands on Emily's shoulders and lightly brushed her cheek with her lips.

Emily felt her limbs turn to water. She almost dropped the box she was carrying and stammered: 'I . . . I've brought your Aunt's dress . . . and I'm . . . sorry not to have seen yo, but we've been that busy. Besides, I couldn't exactly call ... that is ... I ...'

Louise interrupted: 'Come on, I want to introduce you. Emily, this is Mary Grant. Mary . . . Emily Palmer – a very good friend and sympathizer.'

Emily felt hotter still and wished she had more poise. She looked at the stranger with renewed interest. Small trim shape; pale face; thin hands, which felt all skin and bone inside her own chunky palm. Looked as if a puff of wind would blow her away.

'It's always good to meet another comrade,' Mary said, and the voice was pleasingly deep. 'I've heard of your exploit in Birmingham.'

'I'd do it again, given the chance,' Emily said roughly.

Louise took her up sharply: 'You mean that?'

The singing quietened and Emily's heart skipped a beat. Something was coming and things weren't so straightforward any more. With May all set for London she had responsibilities. But she nodded.

'Tell her, Mary.'

'We're planning a continuous speech at a Liberal party meeting. The idea is that everyone chosen to take part learns the speech by heart and one by one we stand up in the audience and interrupt the proceedings. Of course we're bound to be thrown out, but as one goes, there will always be another to carry on.'

'You could do it, Emily. I'm sure you could,' Louise urged. 'I'm going to start the ball rolling.'

From bright red, Emily turned white. 'Me . . . speak?'

'Mary's got it all written out and had copies made. You can even read it if you aren't too good at remembering. Do say you will.'

All this time she had prayed for a chance. When it came it was *talking*! What had happened to her lucky day? And what if she got arrested? It would be another smack in May's face. Mrs Silver would turn her down flat, just like Ma Harris. But you couldn't refuse. There were times when the outside thing was of greater importance.

'All right,' she croaked, and they were the most difficult

two words she had ever spoken.

'Splendid! That's four I've recruited.' Mary fished about in a capacious bag at her feet and took out some foolscap sheets closely typewritten. 'I'll give you two and then if you can interest anyone else, please do so. They can always speak up at the end if we exhaust our planned eight speakers. Don't forget, you will be number five in ♦rder. Now I must go. I've stayed far too long.' She stood up and took Emily's hand again. 'I'm so glad we have met.' It was no ordinary pleasantry. In spite of her turmoil Emily warmed to this bird-like creature. 'Caxton Hall, a week next Thursday, eight-thirty.'

If I ever get away, Emily thought.

'I'll see you out,' Louise said. 'Don't slip away, Emily. I want a word.'

Left alone with her confusion, Emily walked restlessly about the room. What had she let herself in for this time? Louise could charm the skin off a pig. Magic in her somewhere. And beauty. Emily stopped in front of the mirror, staring at her own broad features with distaste. She eyed the hat, all roses and lace. Her navy-blue felt was hideously sensible. Would she look ridiculous – a dog's dinner? With great daring she picked up the hat, exchanging it for her own, securing the hatpins and lowering the veil. The mirror showed fantasy; a stranger reflected there. The brim cast gentle shadows over veiled seductive skin. Peaches and cream. She lifted the netting, and still it was not herself. She was so lost in her dream she didn't know anyone had come into the room until she saw Peter's reflection behind the hat. He was smiling.

'How nice you look.'

Acutely embarrassed, she began pulling out the hatpins, stabbing her thumb in the process.

'No, don't take it off. It suits you.'

Under the influence of his bold admiring stare, she mumbled something about having to go, her hands hovering over the brim.

'Oh, won't you stay for a while? It's such a long time since I saw you. Of course Louise gives me odd bits of news now and again, but it's not the same as live conversation. I want to know how you are liking your job. Is it a good place? And has Louise inveigled you into any more Suffragette schemes?' He seemed genuinely interested, which pleased yet puzzled her. His manner, as always, was composed and there was no hint of mockery, but she felt suspicious all the same. Had he become more concerned for the Cause over these past weeks, or was he merely being pleasant? She didn't want to talk about the plan Louise had in mind; it was much too fresh and alarming.

'The job's all right,' she managed to say.

'And the other thing?'

She laced her fingers together and looked away from him into the summer garden.

'I'm sorry,' he said. 'You don't want to discuss it. I shouldn't probe.'

His quick sensitivity to her feelings made her look back at him and she surprised an unexpected passing tenderness of expression.

Thoroughly disconcerted, she blurted out: 'Are yo on a visit?'

'Shall we say I'm a long-term guest . . . until I get a place of my own. I'm in charge of Father's London office. Quite a reformed character. Between ourselves it's a good deal more convenient for getting out to Hurlingham. I'm shortly to qualify as a fully trained balloon pilot. After that I'll have a dabble at aeroplanes, though they haven't the same attraction for me as balloons.' He looked at her eagerly. 'I know – you'll have to come for a flight some time. How about that?'

'Oh . . . I'm not sure . . .' The very notion filled her with dismay. Up there in the clouds. It wasn't natural. Downright dangerous!

'Do say yes. It would be a splendid lark.'

She couldn't resist a smile which he took for assent, but was really because the phrase was so like Louise's way of talking. She had moved over to the window as a way of covering her embarrassment. Peter followed, brushing against her. The contact shivered down her arm.

'That hat,' he said. 'You look stunning . . . a regular

"Gibson Girl".'

She had seen pictures of them in *Home Notes* and the comparison was patently absurd.

'Yo needs specs if that's what yo thinks.' She was grinning, tickled by the thought of being tall and willowy, but some of the tension had been ousted by a more easy friendliness.

'You don't believe me, do you,' he said, tilting her head upwards. With a jerky movement he dabbed a kiss on her cheek, knocking the hat over one ear.

Instinctively she stepped back.

He was immediately apologetic. 'I beg your pardon. I didn't think you would mind.'

The awful formality killed any hope of saying she didn't mind one little bit and that it was the most wonderful thing that had ever happened and please kiss her again.

Peter took her silence for disapproval. He watched her take off the hat and replace it on the table, seeing anger in her corn-poppy cheeks. For once he could think of no way to smooth over this gaffe.

Emily was wishing frantically that Louise would come back. It seemed six days since she had gone to see Mary Grant to the front door. But when the sitting-room door opened and she came in, her feelings reversed and she longed for more time to sweep away the misunderstanding between Peter and herself.

'Hello, Pete. Didn't know you were back.'

How could she be so ordinary? The room was thick with tight feelings. Didn't she notice anything?

'Uncle Henry's just come in. He said if I saw you to say he wants a word.'

Emily picked up her shabby felt hat and jammed it on her hair. She was halfway to the door when Louise said: 'Where are you off to? We haven't had our talk . . . or any tea for that matter.' She went to the bell by the mantelpiece and pressed the button.

'I'd better go and beard the lion in his den,' Peter said without looking at Emily.

'Come back afterwards and share our tea,' Louise said. Yes . . . oh no! Emily's feelings see-sawed.

'If I'm in one piece after Uncle H. has finished with me.' Peter said with false cheerfulness. 'These interviews are usually unnerving.' He nodded at Emily without actually meeting her eyes. 'Goodbye for the present,' and left without another mention of ballooning.

'Sit down then! You look so uncomfortable standing in the middle of the room.' Louise patted the couch beside her.

Emily sat on the edge, thinking miserably that the gold and silver day seemed to be crumbling round her feet. Why had he spoiled everything? Not that she objected to being kissed, but she did mind the idea that he could only have been flirting.

'You're very quiet,' Louise said. 'Peter been upsetting you?'

Emily shrank. 'Oh . . . no, of course not.'

'That's good then. Now, listen to my scheme for escaping from Aunt Gertrude's clutches on Thursday week.'

10

THE engine slowly drawing the passenger train into Paddington station creaked and groaned, throwing off clouds of gritty steam. Emily looked anxiously along the length of brown and cream carriages for a sight of May's thin little face . . . and there she was!

'Emmie . . . oh, Emmie!' There was enough love poured into her frantic hug and warm never-ending kisses to make up for the months of separation. Flustered and happy, hairpins falling, Emily stared incredulously over the top of May's tam-o'-shanter at Vic!

'Hello, Emmie! Surprised?'

He looked pale, with dark circles under his eyes and, like it always did, his cap had difficulty in sitting on top of his springy hair. She felt her eyes brimming and there was a great lump in her throat.

'Lend us your hanky,' she croaked, and trumpeted into it.

'There's so much to tell,' May said. 'It'll take me at least a year.'

Emily and Vic looked at each other and burst out laughing.

'You'll do!' Vic said. 'Here, give us a hand with this bag, Emmie.'

They hired a four-wheeled 'growler' pulled by a sway-backed horse, Emily insisting it was to be her treat. When they were inside, Vic slipped an arm round her shoulders.

'I'm sorry about your bike. I'd not have sold it if I'd been in work. Mine was hocked weeks back – things have been that tight at home. A chap at Ernie's works give me a fair price for yours. I've still some left. Yo better have it.'

'Don't talk so daft,' Emily said brusquely. 'I've me wages and yo'll be needing that . . . and don't go worrying. I told yo to sell it didn't I? What use have I got for a bike now, living at the place I works?' Not wanting to think about it, she hurried on: 'What brings yo to London?' As if she couldn't guess!

'Work mostly . . . lack of it. The strike at our works is set to go on for weeks and what with Dad off too and Ernie all holier-than-thou, and yo knows how it is with Mam, the house wasn't fit to live in. I thought I'd join the army, but I can do that as well down here as in Brum. Company for May on the journey.'

'And of course Vera never crossed your mind!'

Vic reddened. 'How is she?'

It was on the tip of Emily's tongue to tell him her fears about Vera's health, but she didn't want to make him worry. Time enough for that.

'We've settled in real nice,' she said evasively. 'Mrs Silver is that kind. Tell yo what, we're going to a meeting tonight, Vera and me. Yo could come along too, if yo don't mind a bit of fun and games.'

May shifted forward on the worn seat. 'Suffragette meeting is it?' She was all eyes, agog with excitement.

'A political meeting of the Liberal Party,' Emily said with great solemnity. 'While it lasts! We've got plans.'

'Oh, can I come?'

It was cruel to say no, but there was nothing she could do. The going was likely to be rough and she couldn't risk May getting hurt. 'Next time,' she said rashly, not able to bear the look of awful disappointment. 'Yo needs your beauty sleep tonight, my girl. Mrs Silver will expect a full day's work tomorrow.'

'Will there be trouble tonight?' Vic asked.

'Don't see as there's likely to be an exception this time.'

He was looking at her very seriously. Worried about Vera, no doubt. And she had to admit she was feeling queasy about the business herself. A strong arm might be very welcome. He'd stood up for her in the past.

The 'growler' had left the wide main street and was bumping over cobbles, stopping and starting as the horse threaded through the narrow ways, squeezing past delivery carts, the driver exchanging oaths with barrow boys. Thick succulent smells wafted in through the open window, onion soup, rich gravies, bread baking. The unconscious thought moved forward in her mind. She really did feel at home here. It was getting to be part of her bones.

'Will yo mind if there is a bit of a rough house?' she asked Vic.

'After all these weeks hanging about . . .' the old quirky humour had returned to his face, 'can't wait to have a go!' adding more seriously: 'Yo women have a raw deal. There's too much injustice in this world. I reckon it's time someone made a stand.'

Louise glanced surreptitiously at her watch. Around her the packed theatre buzzed with conversation. Ten minutes to the performance, three-quarters of an hour before the meeting was due to begin. If she was ever to reach Caxton Hall in time she would have to get away soon. Pity she had to turn up in this extravagant evening gown, but it couldn't be helped. The cloak was all-enveloping, heaven be praised. She tapped impatiently on the gilt arm of the chair. Over the front of the box she could see the orchestra down below, tuning up. Any minute now they would burst into the overture. Already there was a murmur of expectation in the audience. Now or never!

'I think I ought to make myself comfortable, before the curtain rises,' speaking into her Aunt's ear.

Behind her fan Aunt Gertrude nodded, frowning just a little at even this oblique reference to anything so indelicate as going to the lavatory. Louise picked up her evening bag, winking at Peter who had seen and interpreted their Aunt's reaction.

Out in the plushy corridor she wasted no time, almost flying down the stairs, collecting her cloak and bundling into a cab called by the commissionaire.

The streets seemed horribly full tonight and the air was warm and sticky, slowing everything down to an infuriating sweaty crawl. Time and again she glanced at her watch, seeing the minutes relentlessly pass. At last they were bowling along the Strand. Aldwych passed, pigeons whirling in Trafalgar Square, Whitehall and the Houses of Parliament – horrible place, full of entrenched outdated ideas! On and on wth the hot city dust drying her nostrils, into Victoria Street narrowly missing a stray cat and then into Caxton Hall. Emily was there. The sight of her solid reliable bulk soothed the butterflies. Mary too, and Vera with a man standing beside her. Something familiar about his face.

'I'm that glad to see yo,' Emily said as Louise paid off the cabby. 'I thought yo'd been prevented from coming after all. I was crossing my fingers and toes!'

'Ready?' Mary asked, murmuring: 'The others have gone in. Best not to be conspicuous.'

Louise squared her shoulders, feeling the butterflies coming back. Breathe deep. Take a leaf out of Emily's book – be calm and practical. Salt of the earth.

How assured she is, Emily was thinking as she watched Louise enter the foyer with a rustle of pink silk over hidden lace frills. I could never be so fearless, not in a month of Sundays.

'Remember to spread out,' Mary reminded them.

'Yo go with Vera,' Emily told Vic. If anyone needed protection Vera would. She'd have to rely on her own tough muscles if it came to a struggle, but being practical only just controlled her nerves. Afterwards she could never give a description of the Hall, except to say that it was big and filled to bursting with a mountain of flesh, which crowded in, a hostile threatening mass. She chose the centre of a row towards the back of the Hall where she would be fairly well protected by bodies from any official wanting to throw her out. People were already filing on to the platform, sitting on the respectable chairs; high collars, watch-chains and bald heads gleaming. A table stood before them, with a carafe of water and glasses. How she longed for a drink. Her throat was dry as a bone.

'Ladies and gentlemen . . .' The chairman was tapping on the table with his gavel. The murmurs quietened. Emily shrank. The meeting had hardly begun, but she felt exposed; sure that everyone must know her intention. In a minute they'd all be turning to stare, before she'd uttered one word. Frantically she scanned the sea of faces for the reassuring sight of Louise, and found her six rows away sitting straight and proud. If she can do it, Emily said inside herself, yo can!

The chairman was working through an introductory speech, which seemed likely to last for six weeks at least. Louise was to stand up as soon as the principal speaker opened his mouth. Reginald McKenna, who had introduced that hated Cat and Mouse Act in Parliament! Emily watched him get to his feet. Smug bastard! Oh God, please let her stomach lie down. He was speaking now, but the thunder in her ears cut out the sound of his voice. She watched Louise get to her feet, unfurling the green, white and purple banner with VOTES FOR WOMEN printed on it. Listen . . . she must listen! The words of the speech she had read a hundred times were rolling from Louise's tongue, her resonant voice filling every corner of the Hall. No reaction; people stunned; even the man on the platform hesitated. A long, long moment.

'Suffragettes!' The cry was picked up in different parts of the Hall, then: 'Shame . . . throw her out!'

Four burly men were making their way down the aisle either side. The men and women seated beside Louise turned on her, snatching the banner. Officials closed in, pushing along the row, treading on toes. There was no escape, but still she went on speaking:

'. . . as the world looks on. It is the shame of England that half its population should be treated thus, denied the privilege as are convicts, and . . .' Her part was done. Half dragged, unresisting, the cloak torn from her shoulders, Louise was hurried into the aisle and ejected from the Hall.

But the speech was not over.

'Convicts and lunatics,' boomed a voice with the power of a foghorn. 'Is this the mark of a mature and well-tried civilization, or will in years to come the finger of scorn and derision be pointed at . . .'

Fury seething and wrestling with her unstable stomach, Emily watched the horsy woman roughly shoved from the body of the Hall. And still the speech was flowing,

Another woman banished, trailing shreds of tulle and veiling. The fourth was Mary Grant, her deep voice compelling attention, conquering the noise of the angry crowd. Emily would be next.

'Give her a taste of the whip,' someone bellowed, but as Mary was grabbed and manhandled from her place, Emily caught another gentler comment from the woman next to her:

'Poor thing . . . it's not right to treat a woman so.'

The voice had gone, lost in her own trembling attempt to shout the words. Emily felt her whole body shaking as if she was suffering from a fever. Her heart was banging about, ready to leap out of her chest and the din in her head was past belief. She stared at the speech.

'. . . be pointed at . . . at Mr Asquith and his so-called *Liberal* Government. Yo may th . . . think their rule democratic, but . . . future generations will pronounce . . . it a tyranny, a dictatorship . . . a monstrous travesty of . . . justice. My friends, yo cannot sit here unmoved. We ask yo all . . .' The words on the paper were coming and going like a flock of sparrows against the sun, impossible to read, nothing like the practised confidence of the others, but keeping going. She was conscious of a little bound of proud happiness. However small and short-lived, she'd not failed.

And then came the blow, a painful crack on her spine which knocked her forward on to the shoulders of two men in front. The paper was torn from her hands and before she had time to recover her breath or attempt to go on speaking, the strong-arm men were on her. Well she'd not go without giving as good as she got. As the first man took a handful of her coat she clenched her fist, careful to keep thumb outside fingers, and lammed for all she was worth into his face. It was a foolish move, she knew it as soon as he let go and covered his face with his hands. Any sympathy there had been hedging her, vanished as blood flowed from his nose. From behind, her hat was knocked off and her hair seized so painfully that she was forced to move in the direction she was being pulled. There were other blows, surreptitious kicks on shins and feet as she staggered over a forest of knees; inexorably dragged outside, where there seemed to be an army of policemen to deal with the handful of women.

Through tears of pain and fury, Emily glimpsed Louise in the grip of a burly policeman. For a moment their eyes met and without a word spoken Emily knew that the façade of cloak-and-dagger adventure had been swept away for ever. It was truth they faced together; the bare fact of physical weakness that seemed to control the destiny of women. She jerked ineffectually, trying to release her pinioned arms. Louise was being half carried, half dragged towards the street and the waiting police van. The doors moved constantly as more women were forced through. Uproar from the Hall came and went in bursts. Emily saw Vera swing her handbag at a policeman and close by Vic was struggling like a madman, shouting oaths that brought the ghost of a grin. His strength and ferocity brought a temporary diversion. The arm which held her like a band of steel relaxed ever so slightly. She didn't waste this heaven-sent chance, but swivelled to face the man, bringing her knee up sharply, seeing him fold with a cry that brought a strange mixture of satisfaction and horror. But she was free! The fighting that surrounded Vic was causing chaos. Several policemen were struggling in a confused tangle of arms and legs and rolling helmets. She looked round for Vera, but could not see her, and in the process of wriggling through the heaving crowd was elbowed in the eye. The blow acted like a spur, putting one thought in her head . . . to escape.

'Don't let that wild-cat get away, George,' someone shouted.

Emily did not stop to find out who George was, but sped along the pavement, past iron railings towards the main road and across with scarcely a look for traffic. There was the close rattle of wheels and a creaking of leather. The hot breath of a horse blew over her cheeks, with the blare of a motor horn and smell of petrol fumes.

'What the bloody 'ell are you up to . . . Tired of life, darlin'?'

Emily hardly saw or heard, racing blindly towards

Victoria station and comparative safety.

It seemed like years later that she reached the brown painted door in Turnbull Street. All sense of time had vanished. Her head ached with a nagging insistence and one eye was almost closed, making the job of putting key in keyhole difficult. The lights were on in the passage and Mrs Silver came out.

'My Gawd . . . whatever happened?'

Emily shook her head, then began shaking with hard dry sobs.

'Here,' Mrs Silver became firm and practical, propelling her along, 'into the kitchen and we'll bathe that eye.' She pushed her on to one of the kitchen chairs, went to the dresser, and took a bottle and glass from the cupboard. 'Drink this first.'

Brandy that wormed down into her stomach, calming the shudders.

'Now then,' said Mrs Silver, 'tell me all about it,' and when Emily finished her tale, added with unexpected vehemence: 'Devils!'

'Yo ain't mad then?'

'Not at you . . . at those bigots sitting up there in the House of Commons with their fat stomachs and self-important airs. Oh . . .' She shook her fist, words being inadequate.

And that, Emily decided, is the most surprising discovery of all in this topsy-turvy day.

'You said Vera went with you?' Mrs Silver asked.

'Yes, but I don't know what happened to her, nor Vic.' A cloud of depression settled round her.

Mrs Silver heaved a great sigh, getting stiffly up from the kitchen chair. 'If it wasn't for my wretched lumbago I'd . . .' She let the sentence hang in the air as she rubbed her back, then went on: 'Too late to do much tonight. I'll go round to the police station in the morning. If there's bail to be had or fines to pay, you needn't worry, my dear. Put it down to my contribution to the Cause.'

11

LOUISE shifted on the sofa and Emily hurried to arrange the cushions more comfortably behind her shoulders. How gaunt and pale she looked with lines of weariness creasing beneath the beautiful eyes. The set of her mouth had changed too, the old light-hearted look was gone. Rage consumed Emily. Those prison beasts! That foul obscene torture!

Mary Grant came into the comfortable shabby sitting-room carrying a tea tray. She set it down on the table by the wall, pulled a chair close to the crackling fire and motioned to Emily.

'I'm so pleased you made time to visit us,' she said. 'We've been talking about you a lot since Louise came out of prison this time. There's a scheme afoot – just up your street . . . but I'm putting the cart before the horse. Tea first, before everything gets cold. I've toasted some muffins and treated us to fresh cream buns.' She looked at Louise. 'Are you comfortable?'

'I'll be easier when my bones are padded a little better,' Louise said ruefully. 'I lost nine pounds last stretch, and I wasn't bonny when I went in.'

'It's vile!' Emily burst out. 'I don't know how yo stands it, chased around all the time. Detectives after yo, ready to pounce as soon as yo shows your face on a platform.'

Louise shrugged. 'Adds spice, you know. Why, I'm quite a celebrity these days. Detective Inspector Mason is specially assigned to hunt me down.' A faint flush tinged her prominent cheekbones and she laughed without any of her former gaiety.

'Now don't bother about that,' Mary said soothingly. 'You are safe enough in my flat. All you have to do for the present is get back your strength. Here, eat one of these lovely stodgy muffins, guaranteed to put weight on the skinniest.'

'But it's a crime! They hunt us like wild animals when it's them that are the beasts.' Emily could not repress her anger which was always ready to boil over since the Caxton Hall meeting. She bit May's head off at the slightest thing and was increasingly scratchy with Vera, who had slid back into her old shell since being in court. Not that she'd had to face prison like Vic or Louise. Poor old Vic, what a fright he'd looked there in the dock! She could see him now, black and blue, nose swollen, split lips – and three months' hard labour as a reward for siding with the Suffragettes! Worse still, Vera hadn't visited him once . . . and *that* made her want to spit! But that was four months ago. Vic had done his time and joined the army since then, Louise had done two stretches and Peter – Peter was working very hard, so Louise said. He might as well have gone to the moon. She hadn't seen him since that awful affair with the hat. It was October now and the future to look to, though she sometimes thought if every window in England was smashed and all the big houses burned, it wouldn't bring them one inch nearer the coveted Vote.

Mary broke into these uncomfortable thoughts. 'There's been some talk at Headquarters of forming a bodyguard to protect Mrs Pankhurst and the other leaders. I know she and Annie Kenney have gone to stay in Paris with Christabel, but they'll be back and with the heat on like it is, they'll need protection.'

'You'd be good at that, Emily,' Louise said.

Mary added: 'The women picked have to be brave enough and have the physique to take punishment.'

'And yo are asking me?' Emily said slowly.

'The way you acquitted yourself at Caxton Hall didn't go unnoticed.'

A flush mounted Emily's cheeks. Old feelings about violence breeding nothing but violence marred the honour. But if she agreed, it would be a job of protection. No striking first blows. It was a laugh anyway to think of her peasant body being something in her favour for once!

'If yo thinks I can do it, I'm willing. Who else will there be?'

'I've got a list somewhere.' Mary went to a little walnut bureau and rooted through the untidy pigeonholes. 'Can't lay my hands on it, but I can tell you that Gertrude Harding is in charge. She's a housemaid most of the time. If you come to Lincoln's Inn House next week you can meet her and learn all the details.'

Action, Emily decided, even violent action, was better than sitting on your backside all day long. She'd done nothing more daring than hurl a piece of hard chalk with the message 'DEATH OR RELEASE' wrapped round it at a doctor's window in Harley Street, since the Caxton Hall fracas. The chalk had bounced harmlessly, dropping down into the area below. It had been a desperate, useless re-action to one of Louise's hunger strikes.

'I could eat another bun,' Louise remarked. She sounded surprised and Emily said:

'At least yo don't have no trouble with bulges. If I was to eat another I'd burst out of my stays!'

They all laughed.

'Who cares about stays anyway?' Mary said. 'Freedom for ever!'

An easy silence settled on them. Emily felt secure – accepted for herself, with none of the old class gap getting in the way. She stayed another half-hour revelling in the quiet companionship. The warm glowing bond lasted as she walked through the piling yellow leaves heaped by an autumn wind on her way home, and stayed with her for days to come.

'No, not like that . . . a firmer grip, so you can twist your opponent this way . . . see?'

Emily took hold of the instructor's jacket and tried again. A sharp twist to the right, body braced, knee out and . . . crash! She found herself sprawling on the tatami mat, remembering just in time how to break her fall, smacking forearms down to take the weight of her body.

'Try again!'

She straightened her loose white jacket and retied the sash, feeling annoyed by her own slow reactions. It wasn't her first ju-jitsu lesson; she ought to be making more headway by now. The instructor, a tiny little woman, smiled encouragingly.

'Don't get downhearted. You'll soon get into the way of it.'

Emily said wryly: 'Yo'd think with all my brawn I'd manage better!'

'Brawn's all very well if you're a wrestler, but in this sport it's skill and timing that count.'

Sport is hardly the word, Emily thought. More like hard labour! They had been training for several weeks, thirty of them, mostly young and beefy like herself. To avoid discovery every session had been held in a different place, sometimes in basement flats of sympathizers to the Cause, sometimes, like tonight, in attic rooms. At the first meeting at Headquarters in Lincoln's Inn House, they had been issued with small Indian clubs which had to be worn under their skirts when on duty. It had all seemed very military.

In the oddly sloping ceiling a large skylight looked down on the bustling exercise below. A dormer window opened from an alcove in one wall. Both were dense and black with threatening fog and the only light came from two round globes of burning gas on the far wall. Emily, on the floor, once more, but this time locked in a struggle for supremacy with a woman even broader than herself, rolled over and saw two faces pressed close against the glass of the skylight. The surprise broke her concentration and she was quickly twisted into a painful armlock.

'No, give over . . .' She was slapping her hand in submission on the mat. 'Stop . . . everybody . . . we're being spied on.'

It took a moment for her message to get through, but when it did someone had the presence of mind to turn out the gas. The room was plunged into gloom filled with flurried whispers. Everyone knew the drill, which was to dress and get away as quickly as possible, but they were all hampered by the almost total darkness. The women were knocking into one another. Someone tripped over Emily's feet and cursed.

Emily slipped her jacket back on top of her dress and

dragged on her coat. Down everlasting stairs, jostling each other with whispered apologies. There was the front door. Cautious now. Try to look casual – don't attract attention.

A series of blinding flashes dazzled and bewildered her. Emily blinked, trying to regain her power of sight. Her heart was beating hard in alarm.

'Police!' A muttered warning in her ear. 'They're taking photos of us.'

The tall old house was situated between two distant gaslamps and a light fog had dimmed the street to a sepia haze. Emily crossed the road and began walking rapidly along the uneven pavement, disconcerted by the idea of her face being on record. The implications were vast and shadowy, but it was no good worrying now. The important thing was to get home unobserved.

She had not gone far before she became aware of footsteps following. She fought down the panic. Anyone could be walking this way. Still, it wouldn't hurt to hurry a little. She turned a corner walking more briskly. The footsteps quickened. Another corner and another. Still the footsteps dogged her, showing no sign of trying to overtake. She realized with a stab of dismay that whoever it was, intended tracking her to her own doorstep. And that really would be disaster, because she would not only betray herself, but Vera and Mrs Silver as well. There was nothing for it, she would have to shake off his attentions. A little farther along the street was a newsagent's shop. It was a fine opportunity to take stock of her pursuer.

'Evening News, please.' As the man behind the counter took her money, Emily positioned herself close to the door, pretending to glance at a magazine. Yes, there he was under the gaslamp, a man of medium height in a macintosh and bowler hat, lighting his pipe as a pretence for stopping. Without doubt a policeman. She rolled the newspaper. It made a handy light weapon. Coming out of the shop she set off at a good pace towards the road junction where trams rattled on their way to the Embankment. Reaching this haven luck was with her and she was able to jump on to a tram just as it moved away from the stop. She sank breathlessly on to the wooden bench, but she had reckoned without her pursuer. He sprinted the last few yards, springing on to the footboard with the agility of a monkey. Emily unrolled the newspaper and pretended to read. What was she to do? The conductor came to take her fare and she paid for several stops farther than she intended travelling, knowing that this was only a faint hope. Close by Cleopatra's Needle with the yellow mist coming in drifts off the Thames, she got up and skipped off the tram as it halted behind a cab. The detective followed.

What now?

She walked quickly, keeping in the shadow of the Embankment wall, wishing the mist would turn into an all enveloping pea-souper, but a light drizzle had already started, washing away that hope. At least there were more people about. If she crossed over and went up Villiers Street perhaps there was a chance of losing him in Charing Cross station. Night life had started. Lights glittered out over the wet pavements where a few street women were already hanging about. There was plenty of noise and bustle inside the station, but infuriatingly, not enough of a crowd to act as a screen. Ladies-room or station buffet? The ladies-room offered greater privacy, but there was no other way out and it was only shelving the problem, not solving it. What on earth was she going to do? She might at least treat herself to a sandwich and a cup of tea and take the weight off her aching feet.

She took her food and tea to a table where she could see who came in by looking in the wall mirror, at the same time keeping her back to the door. You had to admit he was good at his job, she thought when he walked in a minute later. She heard him say: 'Cup of tea please, miss,' to the woman behind the counter. There was a mild quality about his voice which made her feel that in other circumstances she would like him. She was tempted to go and sit at his table as a piece of cheek, but that would be even more dangerous a game than the one they were already playing. Instead she drank her tea slowly and chewed the sandwich which was stale and tasted of sawdust. Behind the counter the woman was plainly getting ready to go home. The breathing space was over. Picking up her newspaper, Emily walked out into the station yard, wearily aware of the all too solid shadow behind. Slowly she plodded across Trafalgar Square, up the steps, threading through traffic too sparse now for shelter. St Martin-in-the-Fields rose bulky and protective, but that too would only offer brief respite. She was beginning to despair of ever getting home. One thing she knew for certain was her determination not to betray the others. If she had to walk all night she would do just that. If only her strength lasted. Already she felt exhausted. A long day at work, then hard physical exercise was no preparation for a night on the tiles.

She was about to give herself a pep talk about the importance of keeping morale high when she saw the uniformed policeman slowly pacing towards her, on the pavement opposite. Without pausing, Emily shot across the road and as luck would have it, the detective was forced to wait on the kerb for a knot of traffic to pass. In these few heaven-sent seconds she ran to the policeman.

'Please help me,' she begged, trying to be feminine and appealing. 'I'm being followed by that man over there,' pointing.

'Don't you fret, miss.' The policeman responded in a most fatherly way. 'You get along. *I'll* deal with that customer.'

'Oh thank you, constable!' There was no need to feign gratitude, it fairly bubbled out of her, and without waiting any longer she ran along the pavement, nipping back across the road and into a side street. The reprieve was brief, but at least it gave her a chance and after running a few more yards she turned into an alley she would normally never have dared enter. There, in a dark doorway, she flattened herself, turning her head away so that even the whiteness of her face could not attract attention. In the distance, getting nearer, she heard the running footsteps, two sets this time. She hardly dared breathe as they passed the end of the narrow alley, exploding the night. As the sounds died she was overcome with weakness. Her knees shook and her body kept twitching. Gradually strength seeped back. No time now for weakness or she would lose the valuable advantage.

It was impossible not to keep looking back over her shoulder, but as she wove through a labyrinth of streets, coming ever closer to Soho and home, without a sign of either policeman, her spirits bounced up and she began to giggle. It really was funny. Set a sprat to catch a mackerel, or were they both mackerel? Who cared . . . she'd fooled them both!

She was still grinning to herself as she felt for her key, secure in the knowledge she was safe.

'Emily?'

She spun round. It was Peter! The sight of him was enough to tip the world upside down. An incredible finish to a crazy evening. She was in such a whirl it didn't occur to her to wonder why he was there.

'I've been waiting a long time,' he said.

'For me?' It was a stupid question, but served to shelter her feelings.

'Vera said you were out. I calculated it wouldn't be for the whole night. She wasn't forthcoming about when you'd be back.'

Emily waited, conscious of aching feet and an empty dragging feeling in her stomach. Why didn't he get to the point?

'It isn't something we can discuss on the doorstep and I realize it is far too late for you to ask me in. Will you come and sit in the car? It's parked round the corner.'

She stared at him uneasily. Certainly no one would question a girl and a man together at night in this area. It was a common enough sight. As for trusting him . . . Reluctantly she moved away from the door.

'I want to know where Louise is living,' he said bluntly as soon as they were in the car.

'Don't yo know?' She was astonished.

'I'd hardly be asking you if I did.'

There seemed no sense to be made of it. Why hadn't Louise told him she was staying with Mary Grant? Unless

. . . unless she was afraid he might tell Old Man Marshall. But she couldn't believe *that*! There was such a bond between brother and sister – quarrelsome, but close.

'If she don't choose to tell you, then it's not for me to say,' Emily said slowly.

'But that's ridiculous!'

'No it ain't . . . it's common sense.'

'Come now, I have to know. It's important.'

'It's important she gets rest and quiet to build up her strength. One careless word and she'd be back inside before yo could say knife, and I ain't going to betray her.'

'It's not a question of betrayal.' He was obviously exasperated. 'I'm family.'

She didn't know what to do. Sitting so close to him didn't help. Her thoughts were in a tangle and she was so tired.

'Emily, you must tell me!' he almost commanded.

'Oh stop being so . . . so . . . high and mighty!' she snapped.

Whatever reaction she might have expected, it was not the laughter that came bellowing out. She stared at him, taken aback, then gave him a nudge.

'Ssh! Yo'll wake the neighbourhood.' But it was police she was thinking about.

'No laughing matter,' he said after the outburst. 'I'd not ask you if it wasn't urgent. I'd never try and make you betray a trust. But you are my only hope. Lou hasn't written since the Caxton Hall affair when Father told her not to come back home. I tried to smooth things over, visited her in prison and offered to pay her fine, but she's as pig-headed as he is. Two of a kind! And now Father's had a stroke; can't speak. If he could he'd no doubt refuse to go back on his word, but I know in his heart he wants to see her before he dies.'

All the fight went out of Emily. 'He ain't going to get better?'

Peter shrugged. With his face in shadow it was impossible to read his expression, but the hard fact of death shrank everything else to pin-point insignificance, leaving her without the right to refuse.

'Yo know she's on the Cat and Mouse rack?' Oh why didn't he move so the gaslight would show her what he was thinking?

A pause.

'I didn't know.'

'She's out of prison, like I said, but they want her back. If I tell yo the police might find out where she is.'

'So that's what you think of me.'

Emily was appalled. She had only meant to show what danger lay in wait for Louise. To have him think she imagined he would tell the police, was intolerable. The old bogy of speechlessness drove out any method of putting things right.

As if he guessed, Peter took her hand. The contact was all and more than the longest conversation.

'You will tell me!' he said.

'Yes.'

Her hand was squeezed, kissed, then released in quick succession, bringing her to the verge of tears.

'I'd better take yo, so as there won't be no misunderstandings,' she said gruffly. 'But not tonight, in the morning.' And thank God for May with her skilful needle. If it weren't for her and Mrs Silver's backstage devotion to the Cause, she'd have been sacked long ago for all the time off. It was bound to get worse too, now she was one of the Bodyguard. She shivered.

'Cold?' Peter asked.

'Someone must have walked over my grave!' Prison would be a grave. A living death, and it was coming, no doubt about that. She was so afraid. All the violence, where was it getting them? Her thoughts were bound up with fighting in one form or another, and what was the use? 'It's time I went in,' she said, firmly pushing away the fears.

'I'll call round tomorrow then. What time?'

'Make it eleven. We shan't be noticed at that time of day.' She'd square things with Mrs Silver; work all night if need be.

They walked back to the door.

'Good night,' he said. 'And thank you.'

She could see his face now. He looked serious and reserved. A very long way from her, and she hated that.

'Good night!' She unlocked the door and hurried upstairs. There was a gulf between them big enough to hold the Houses of Parliament, Buckingham Palace and the Albert Hall rolled into one. Besides, she had no spare time for falling in love, and with a face like the back end of a tram, she wasn't born for it either. It was golden people like Louise who could go starry-eyed and not look fools.

'Daft as a March hare yo are, Emmie Palmer,' she said aloud.

In the corner bed May stirred. 'What yo say?' Her voice slurred with sleep.

'Nothing that matters.'

'It's nice when yo're back, Emmie.' May woke a little more. 'Was it fun? Did yo get chased?'

'Sh . . . go back to sleep. I'll tell yo all about it in the morning.' Emily pulled the bedclothes round her ears making a protective nest.

'Emmie!'

'Mm?'

'I think yo're that brave!'

Emily didn't answer, but lay quite still wishing very hard that she didn't feel so much of a hypocrite.

12

For the fifth time in ten minutes Emily looked at the wall clock, seeing the pendulum swing with a maddening rhythm that seemed to be holding back time. With an enormous sigh she tried to concentrate on the inset lace she was stitching into a brown satin blouse.

'No good clock-watching, my dear,' Mrs Silver said. 'Best way to make time go slowly. Besides, we don't know when she will get here.'

'Only three hours to go. We'll never get to the Hippodrome in time,' Emily fretted.

It was early April now, April 1914. A charity performance in aid of 'Distressed Gentlewomen' was today's disguise for the W.S.P.U. meeting. Mrs Pankhurst was to have been there, but she had not yet recovered from the awful battering she had received at the Glasgow meeting back in March. Emily still shuddered at the recollection. The cruelty and bloodshed of it lived on in her nightmares. A sick satisfaction came with the sly memory of wielding her bodyguard's club with drastic effect. She had left a good few bruises back in Glasgow and had been lucky to escape arrest. There had been a lull since then with so many leaders ill, in prison or fled from the country. She had not even had contact with Louise, except for a brief note from Peter telling her that they had both returned to Birmingham and their father was not expected to live more than a few days, until the message brought by a total stranger with the news that Louise would be at Turnbull Street on the following Thursday. No mention of time or how she would escape police detection. She was still on their wanted list. The message also said that a member of the Actresses' Franchise League would call that same day to disguise Louise and Emily as Vaudeville artists for the risky journey across the Thames into the heart of south-east London. The actress was here already, sitting close to the fire, warming her hands; personality overflowing into the workroom. Miss Feather and May were all eyes, mesmerized by the gaunt cheekbones and heavy eyelids.

'How about "The Birmingham Belles" for a title?' the actress suggested.

Emily shook her head. 'A bit too near home. Something less obvious.'

'How about . . .' May began and was interrupted by the door-knocker echoing loudly through the house.

Emily was on her feet, running up the stairs and along the hall. The door open, she paused for a fraction of a moment. The middle-aged figure in heavy mourning could not be Louise.

'Lady Grandison to see Mrs Silver,' said the personage, sweeping past Emily into the hall. 'And look lively, Emily!' Once the door was closed, the veil was lifted and Emily was gathered up and soundly kissed on both cheeks. 'You should see your face,' Louise said and began laughing.

'Yo looked like a widow,' Emily blurted out. 'All that black crêpe!'

'An orphan,' Louise corrected.

'Oh . . . yes, sorry . . . I wasn't thinking.'

Louise brushed aside the sympathy as if it touched on another life that had ceased to exist. 'Father died two weeks ago. So now there is nothing to prevent me getting back to work.' She moved on to the workroom, finally closing the subject.

'Why, Miss Marshall!' Mrs Silver said as if it were an ordinary day. 'We are all ready for the fitting.'

Louise looked round the room. 'Oh you don't know how good it is to be back. I feel as if I've been in prison all these months.' The irony did not seem to strike her.

'Tell us how yo got here safe,' Emily begged.

'Did a bit of dressing up in Peter's clothes,' Louise said. 'Pete and I travelled by car as male companions till just outside London, then we stopped and I changed into all this stuff. When we reached Holland Park and Aunt Gertrude's, Pete bundled me into a cab. And here I am.'

Emily felt her heart behaving in a stupidly erratic way

at the mention of Peter. The strong barrier she had built round her emotions suddenly dissolved, leaving her weak and exposed. Her cheeks flamed. Surely they must notice. But everyone was crowding round Louise. Even Vera was showing interest. The actress had opened the handcase she had brought with her and was arranging a collection of jars and greasepaint on one of the tables.

'We were just discussing a possible name for your act,' she said.

'All arranged!' Louise sounded surprised. 'Haven't you seen the programme? "Emmie and Lou, Plenty of Patter, with Songs at the Piano".'

Emily couldn't help laughing in spite of the dangers of using their own names. 'Looks as if I'm left with the songs then,' she said.

'Rubbish! I've heard you speak out. Remember Caxton Hall?'

'If you like to come through to the fitting-room, ladies,' Mrs Silver said, picking up a feather boa and a large hat trimmed with ostrich plumes. 'The costumes are already in there.'

Emily and Louise gazed at one another with ill-concealed amusement as the cab taking them to the Hippodrome wove through tangled traffic towards Vauxhall Bridge.

'You look like a bird of paradise,' Louise said.

'Jackdaw more like, or a magpie. I feels just like a housemaid who's nicked some of her mistress's clothes. Talk about ridiculous! Beauty and the Beast, that's what it is, only the beast was a man and I'm not.'

'Oh nonsense! You've got a bee in your bonnet about your looks.'

'A side of beef with hair on top . . . untidy at that,' Emily moaned with some sincerity inside the jokes.

Louise stopped smiling. 'I believe you mean it.'

'Well, I've got eyes.'

'With the blinds drawn. Pete says you remind him of the country; haymaking and jars of cider and bees buzzing round cornfield poppies.'

'A regular peasant,' Emily said in confusion, hardly

knowing how to take this description. It was funny if nothing else. She didn't even like the country. There weren't enough people for comfort. But at least Peter thought of her sometimes; even talked about her.

'Not far now,' Louise said.

Outside the cab windows the mean streets softened under spring sunlight. A leftover March wind blustered about, hurling litter and skimming the hats of the unwary. There was an edge to the day, stringing Emily's nerves to a high pitch of excitement. Although she would not be officially on duty as a bodyguard, she had taken the precaution of bringing her Indian club. It pressed against her thigh, hanging by a cord under the folds of the loud green dress she was wearing. Louise's dress was white with a purple sash, colours that combined to hint at W.S.P.U. sympathies. But it was the hat Louise wore that delighted Emily most. White roses piled over the crown, large brim edged with white velvet and hazed in fine net. It was the hat of hats. Even more delectable than the one she had tried on at Aunt Gertrude's. But no time now for those thoughts.

'The posters will be up,' she said, pulling away from the memories. 'D'yo think the police will have found out it's a W.S.P.U. meeting?'

'I expect so. They have spies everywhere, or did have. I've been away so long I'm out of touch. You ought to know more than I do.' Louise peered out of the window. 'We'll soon find out. My God, look at them!'

The cab pulled up not ten yards from the Gothic mass of the theatre. Crowds already thronged the pavement under the wrought-iron canopy and around them was a line of policemen. The doors into the foyer were open and a detective stood either side, carefully scrutinizing every person as they passed inside.

Emily's pulses were racing and her heart knocking against her ribs like a coal pick. 'We'll never get past them!'

Louise leaned forward calling to the cabby: 'Stage door if you please!'

The cab moved off, wheeling round the corner into a

dingy street full of flyblown shops.

'That's as far as I can git, miss,' the cabby said.

'Nemesis,' Louise whispered. 'Brace yourself.'

'It's a mercy we're larded up with paint,' Emily muttered. 'If I grin it'll crack! Here goes.'

They got out of the cab and paid the driver. Every poster on the theatre walls had been pasted over during the night and proclaimed:

WOMEN'S SOCIAL AND POLITICAL UNION

VOTES FOR WOMEN

Men and Women hear the truth at
a meeting in the Hippodrome today
Thursday (April 1914) at 3 p.m.
Speeches will be given by:

ANNIE KENNEY
MARY GRANT
LOUISE MARSHALL

Entertainments in aid of funds

'Songs at the piano then!' Emily said.

'If there's a chance!'

They went down the alley which backed the theatre and led to the stage door. Plainclothes men were there too.

'Just a minute, miss!'

Emily recognized the detective who had pursued her after the ju-jitsu lesson. She would never pass his scrutiny!

Her breath came fast and shallow.

'Admirers allowed after the performance, not before, darlin',' Louise said in an unrecognizable cockney voice.

'That's enough of that, miss. We all know this is no show.'

'You may think not, but we've been hired to do our song and dance routine . . . a few jokes thrown in. All good clean stuff mark you, so mind out of the way, 'cause we've got to get changed.'

Emily saw the sandy eyebrows go up. She wound the feather boa high up her neck to shelter her face. In for a penny in for a pound! 'Enjoy the show, love,' she said, and pushed past into the echoing back-stage gloom.

A tall woman with a strong face and protruding eyes, whom Emily recognized from earlier meetings, advanced on them, pretending they were strangers.

'And you are?'

'Emmie and Lou,' Louise didn't forget her accent, which was fortunate as a police constable was stationed inside the stage door.

'Ah yes . . . this way. Number two dressing-room.'

Solitude was there along with a trestle table and a cracked mirror. A few hairpins lay scattered on the floor-boards and a forgotten towel hung on a peg. Around them old smells of greasepaint, size and dust pressed home the strangeness of everything. Emily and Louise stood looking at one another, caught up in shared unspoken emotions. A moment of truth. Whatever speeches were made or left unsaid they knew there was little hope of escape. Oh God, don't let me betray her, Emily prayed. The fear that dogged her at every meeting was back. She'd fight with the best, take any blows, but it was the horror of prison that made her sweat with fear. She took Louise's hands seeking strength.

'I'll be in the wings. If there's trouble I've got my friend.' She patted her skirt.

'If there's any trouble,' said the tall woman coming in and shutting the dressing-room door behind her, 'they're in for a surprise. Barbed-wire,' she added in a whisper. 'In the ivy and flowers at the front of the stage.'

Louise blew out her cheeks. 'It's war all right. Is Mary here and Annie?'

'Mary yes, but so far no sign of Annie.'

'Well if it's only two of us we'll just have to spin out our speeches.'

The tall woman smiled encouragingly. 'You've a good audience. The house is packed.'

From a distance came the sounds of singing: 'Why are we waiting . . . oh why are we . . .'

'Give me the cold cream, Emmie. I must get this muck off my face or no one will know me.'

'I'll be off then, comrade. Mary will begin the proceedings, but it will be better if you both come on stage together. Good luck!'

'We'll need it,' Louise said fervently and took off her hat.

From the wings among a group of Suffragettes, Emily had an oblique view into the auditorium. Lights glittered over gilt and red plush. The singing had died and a hum of expectation tightened the atmosphere to breaking point. A cheer had come bursting out as Mary and Louise went on stage. Mary had held up her hand asking for patience for a few minutes until the principal speaker should join them. And now they were waiting, one minute . . . two . . . Perhaps Annie had been arrested before ever getting here. Perhaps an accident . . .

The heavy blue curtain behind Mary and Louise slowly looped up and a frail skeleton of a woman with large blue eyes sunk in smudged hollows above cheekbones sculptured by hunger and pain, stepped slowly forward. The impact on the audience was enormous. They roared their appreciation for this heroine who time after time had braved hunger, thirst and torture for the sake of the Cause. Emily cheered with them, tears pouring down her cheeks. For of them all her heart went out to this mill girl, a working woman like herself. Once before she had heard Annie speak. This time the North Country voice was the same, but the change in appearance confirmed Emily's worst fears.

'My friends, I want to thank you from my heart for

coming today. You know what you face, what we all have to face, and time may be short for speech-making. So I will come to the point. I am here not to complain about the treatment which I and many other women have received and are still receiving in prison, terrible though it is, but to beg for your support in persuading a misguided government into seeing the error of its ways and so giving Votes to Women. It is only common justice and common sense to allow . . .'

'Arrest that woman . . . all of them . . .'

Adrenalin tensed Emily's muscles as police came from all sides, closing in on the stage. In the wings more police converged. Through a slit in her skirt pocket Emily released her club. Just let them try, that's all! Behind her someone shouted: 'Let me go . . .' and she felt herself roughly pushed aside as two strapping policemen made for the stage.

'Oh no yo don't!' She swung the club, joyfully feeling the strength of her arm. It clipped one man just above the ear.

'Bleedin' hell-cat!' he yelled and turned on her with such ferocity that in a calmer moment she would have shrunk back. This time a surge of delight in the relief of action made her swing at him again, half her attention snatched by the curses and shouts of men caught in the barbed-wire.

'Run, Lou!' she bellowed, as the policemen grabbed an arm and jerked it back. The pain was bad, but she struggled to see if Louise had escaped, bringing her knee up as she had done before. The man grunted, but hung on, seizing the neck of her dress. There was a harsh rending and she wrenched to one side in time to see Louise, hair tumbling, her beautiful hat trodden underfoot, pinioned in the grip of another policeman. She was drumming helplessly with her heels, while Mary Grant was being pulled backwards away from her. Of Annie there was no sign. The momentary break in attention cost Emily dear. Her opponent shifted behind, locking her arms to her sides and gripping her breasts, squeezing and twisting until she thought she must faint from pain. She strove to break his hold, desperately trying to adjust her position with all the skill she had learned, but it was no good. Slowly, inexorably, she was swung off her feet and bundled away from the flailing umbrellas of the roaring rioting audience, through the wings, out via the stage door into the alley and along to a waiting police van. Helplessly she was flung inside, cracking her head on the side of the vehicle. There were other women crouched in the stuffy gloom. Somebody was crying quietly. Rubbing her head, Emily pulled herself into a sitting position.

'Sorry,' she said as her foot caught a leg.

'No matter.'

She could see better now and peered at the woman she had kicked.

'Vera?'

'Emmie . . . oh Emmie I'm so pleased it's you.'

'But I didn't even know yo were coming. Yo never said.' She hotched close and put an arm round Vera, hearing the wheezy breathing that every now and then broke into coughs.

'Came with that actress . . . spur of the moment. I'd been thinking . . . a long time.' She stopped, then went on with a rush: 'I'm a coward, Emmie. That's the long and the short of it. You don't know how I admire all of you who make a stand for your beliefs. But being afraid . . . it's like a maggot eating your insides. In the end I couldn't bear it and when Mrs Silver said "Go on, have the time off, I'd go myself if my back would let me", I made up my mind I'd be like you and Miss Marshall. I'd not run away . . .' The coughs began again, taking her words.

Emily held her gently. 'Yo don't know how good it is to know someone else is as scared as me.'

'You . . . scared . . . too?'

'Ready to pee myself with fright!'

'Emmie Palmer . . . really!'

Painfully conscious of her battered ribs, Emily began to laugh at this final absurdity. How proper Vera was, and yet wasn't she one of the bravest, having more fear than most to overcome? But it was the fact she was shocked that tickled. Emily was still chuckling when the doors opened again and two more women were shoved in; elbows and knees and flying skirts, shunting her closer to Vera.

'Take 'em away!'

There was a jolt and the van bumped uncomfortably over the cobbled road. Emily took hold of Vera's hand. Strangely, she could not look into the bleak future because her mind was entirely filled with a picture of the battered white hat. It seemed almost the cruellest thing.

13

OUT there in the free world the sun is shining, Emily told herself in an effort to bring back some sense of reality. But it did no good. From the moment she and all the other prisoners had been herded into the dark passages of Bow Street Police Court, life had shifted into a world of fantasy. The night they had spent in the cells had been strange, but somehow it was still part of real life. Here was no-man's-land, where all fifty-six of them, battle-scarred men and women, would be dealt with in batches of six. And now it was her turn. She looked over the iron railings of the dock at the crowded courtroom. A hand was waving from the cramped standing space near the door, but in the sea of faces it was impossible to recognize anyone. The press were below the dock, alternately staring and jotting notes on pads of white paper. Court officials in rusty black leaned together in droning groups. On her left was the witness-box with a strange canopy like a rain shelter and in front, presiding over everything, was the carved table and tall empty chair of the magistrate.

From the other end of the dock Louise leaned forward and winked.

'How can she be so cheerful?' Vera whispered. 'I want to die.'

'Don't give in now. It's all a lot of tripe!' Emily was suddenly indignant.

On the other side of Vera, a broad sympathetic girl who had shared bodyguard with Emily, gave Vera a nudge. 'Cheer up, darlin'. All this is good advertisement. We'll get our turn for a say and everyone'll have to listen.'

'But it doesn't make any difference!' Emily's indignation was growing.

'All stand!' called the clerk of the court and was answered with the shuffle of feet and a winding down of conversation.

A *man* to decide our fate, Emily was thinking bitterly as the magistrate settled his several chins and ample stomach into the chair. They were all men in charge, the whole lot of them – so much for justice! Any men on their side weren't in this court.

Their names were read out and police evidence against them hurriedly presented. Out of the stilted phrases grew an unrecognizable picture of events that was supposed to tell of the Hippodrome meeting. Emily clenched her fists. Lies, all of it! Facts so distorted you'd think the Suffragettes had advanced like an army instead of being set upon and beaten.

Louise stood up: 'Sir, may I ask to be allowed to make a statement?'

'You may not.'

'Sir, it is only comomn justice to hear both sides of a dispute.'

The magistrate frowned. 'Be quiet, miss! If we need evidence from you, we shall ask for it.'

'I demand to be heard,' Louise said, striking the rail. 'I will be heard as the Law of England allows. It is only that the Scales of Justice are weighted against women that prevents . . .'

The magistrate raised his voice: 'I told you to be quiet! You are doing yourself nothing but harm.'

Louise did not stop, but speaking more loudly, covered his interruption. 'That prevents truth from being heard in this court and . . .'

'Silence, young woman!' bellowed the magistrate.

One of the policemen guarding the entrance to the dock came up and taking Louise by the shoulders, forcibly sat her down on the wooden bench. Unable to bear any more, Emily jumped up shouting:

'Shame . . . shame! You ain't fit to try us. Yo're no more than a lot of bloody stuffed shirts!'

'Votes for Women!' Louise called, and from the restless courtroom the cry was taken up:

'Votes for Women . . . Votes for Women . . .'

'Oh it was worth it,' Louise said, pacing up and down the passage outside the Bow Street open cells, ' "The Law is a Ass" . . . and didn't we show it up!'

'A six weeks' sentence, *and* in the third division like common criminals,' Vera muttered.

'Who cares! We'll never do it all anyway. I bet you five bob we'll be out in less than a week.'

Emily, sitting on the stone steps which led out of the dark underworld of the police courts, felt the last vestige of excitement generated by the courtroom farce slide away. She was left with the terrifying knowledge that hunger and thirst were the key to the prison doors. That and torture. Would she ever be able to go through with it? She looked at Louise. Two bright spots of colour burning on her cheeks were the only indication of tension. She smiled and patted Emily's shoulder.

'Every stretch in prison brings us closer to winning the Vote.'

Emily smiled back, determined not to betray her inner cowardice.

'Sacrifice for success!' Louise whispered in her ear when the time came for parting. A brief kiss and she was led away.

'Sacrifice for success.' Emily repeated the words to herself when she was bundled into the Black Maria with the others – twelve of them, in separate coffin-like compartments with barely enough room to turn round. Last in, Emily had a little more of the fresh air than the others and a view through the barred window. Like cattle on the way to market, only the end of the journey wouldn't bring the relief of open pens. And what a journey! Endless jolting through squalid streets that reminded her of home. Some folk spend all their lives in places like this, Emily was thinking with the compassion born of firsthand knowledge, when she heard the cheering. People lined the streets, her sort of people, toilworn and poor. They had come out on to the pavements just to encourage the prisoners whoever they were, and in her stuffy box, Emily wept. From another compartment a woman began singing:

'Shout, shout, up with your song! Cry with the wind, for the dawn is breaking,
March, march, swing you along. Wide blows our banner and hope is waking . . .'

Emily gulped back her tears, struggling after the familiar words, husky at first then gathering strength as Ethel Smyth's rousing tune caught her up. The music lasted all the way to the turrets and mock battlements of Holloway gaol, holding up her spirits as the huge gates closed behind them.

'Emily Palmer, six weeks.' The woman officer wearing a holland dress and dark-blue bonnet, took a key from the bundle hanging on a chain round her waist and unlocked a small dark cubicle. She jerked her head, indicating Emily should go inside. There was terror in this airless place. A small glass spyhole in the door had mercifully been left uncovered and she pressed close, watching the others called and then shut away, and the wardress working down the line of doors with a list of questions.

'Profession?'

'Seamstress,' Emily said.

'Religion . . . can you read . . . write . . . ?' The enquiry went on and on. More prisoners arrived and more. The cubicles were close packed now, lonely terror giving way to sweaty discomfort.

'Like bloomin' sardines,' said one of Emily's companions.

'Better than solitary,' another remarked. 'Last stretch I did I had four days in the punishment cell. That was an experience and a half, I can tell you!'

In front of the doctor Emily unbuttoned her dress. The stethoscope was cold on her breast and there was no warmth in the question: 'Are you all right?'

Later in the dank pitted bath a little comfort crept back, but it was short-lived when she was told briskly to get out and dress; a scratchy business in the ill-fitting lumpy clothes. She pulled up the red and black striped wool stockings. They'd have to stay up by strength of will, there was nothing else! White arrows on the dark-green dress, black ones on the dingy blue and white check apron; a white cap with strings tying under the chin. Her shoes didn't match and the laces were broken, making walking through the long halls a difficult task.

It was a barn of a building. Filing through the echoing blocks, they saw tier upon tier of landings, like shelves, surrounding a central open space. Flights of black iron steps connected them and all were enclosed by iron trellis screens. Between the landings of the first floor, wire netting was strung to prevent any attempt at suicide.

Emily eyed the rows of anonymous doors. The prospect of learning all too soon what lay behind them brought a cold queasiness to her stomach. She could see Vera a little way in front, head bowed, shoulders shaking from time to time as she coughed. Of Louise she had seen nothing since they parted at Bow Street. They clattered up a stairway, the sounds blending with cries from other prisoners into a weird chorus. The march went on, pausing at a small office to collect sheets, a Bible, a tract called 'The Narrow Way' and a hymn book. Then began repeated stops as each prisoner was put inside a cell.

'Courage, comrade,' someone called as the door closed on Emily.

Courage! Where was it now with the terrible blank door no more than a seam in the wall? The fact that there was no handle brought a black despair which muffled her so close she felt she must suffocate; she opened her mouth gasping for air. The walls closed in. The high ceiling was surely inches nearer? Above the door a recessed gas jet shed thin light. The panic was unbearable, cutting out thought, hope, air ... With her head swimming, Emily forced herself to look round the cell, mechanically naming the objects she saw in a desperate attempt to regain control of herself.

'Bed-boards, shelves, mattress, bedding, wooden spoon, yellow soap, hairbrush, comb, tin mug, watercan, wash basin, slop pail ...' She compelled herself to list them all, thankful to find breathing easier, the iron bands relaxing. From a small barred window too high to see through, came a weak shaft of sunlight. In her trembling fear it seemed a single link with hope. Out there, beyond the stone walls and endless locked doors, was real life and one day she would join it again.

'Not finished yet, 13? Where's your pint?' The wardress, a bony woman with a widow's peak and cheese-grater voice, spoke sharply.

Emily slowly got up from her knees and the floor she had been scrubbing. The cell walls were curving like sea waves and she was forced to clutch at the corner shelf to stop herself from falling.

'Supper not touched nor cleared away? Slovenly habits, 13. You'd best look sharp about it or you'll get no gruel.' It was customary to have plate and pint mug clean and shining, ready on the little cloth for breakfast, so there was more than a hint of kindliness in being given this second chance. But Emily shook her head. 'Stubborn, eh? You'll do yourself no good. Eat and drink a morsel or you know what'll happen.'

Emily closed her eyes, wanting no contact for fear her resolution might weaken. Two nights and a day since she had taken food or drink. An eternity. The scummy cocoa in her mug tempted like the best of Mam's tea and the stale brown bread looked more succulent than those meat balls of Mrs Silver's. Would she ever hold out? She must ... must ...

'Can't stand here all day. If you insist on this foolishness, you know what you'll get.' With this dark threat the wardress slammed out into the landing, turning the key on hope with a cold rattle of metal.

Weak and ashamed, Emily slumped on the stool and sobbed. Her head ached and there was a curious rushing noise in her ears. Tears channelled on to her parched lips, their wet saltiness stinging the cracked skin. Oh sod it ... sod all of them, those blown-up barrels of self-important parliamentary muck! She'd not give in. There was still enough moisture in her to make tears, so she wasn't going to die just yet. But there was the day to get through and another and another. Louise had said they would be out in a week, but there was the torment of Hell to go through before then. Don't look into that pit. One thing at a time. Scrub the floor, then get on with sewing that shirt. The liquid in the mug pulled with all the power of a whirlpool. She stretched out longing hands, held it, brought it nearer, then with a cry hurled the contents over the freshly washed floor.

It began with a single buzz, more of a whisper than anything. A musty reek of ageing herbs came from the knotty pillow under Emily's head. She opened her eyes into a darkness where the pains in her body were magnified into a gigantic all-over toothache. The buzz came again, louder this time, soaring and swooping.

Silence.

Mouth dry and cracked as the Sahara Desert, tongue swollen. There was a crystal-clear spring coming out of the mountainside, pouring over rocks, bubbling with little splashes between pebbles that glinted in the fresh sunlit air. Someone had spread a white cloth embroidered with cherries and apples, but they were changing from stitches into perfect fruit and behind was a tureen, blue and white china, the lid removed, allowing the steam smelling of rich garlic gravy to drift round her head.

With a jerk she was thumped into wakefulness. What was it? Another thud and another! The grey square filtered a little light and now she could see it, a humble bee crashing with desperate urgency against the glass pane. Like herself, a prisoner. She covered her head, trying to blot out sight and sound, but it went on and on until it occupied the whole of her head. She lumbered out of bed, her limbs obeying from a great distance. On the shelf beside her soap and brush was a paper bag which held cotton and thimble. She tipped them out, then with heavy stumbling caution stood on the stool. Careful . . . slide it nearer, nearer! The bee took off, skimming her head, circling the cell, then back again, drawn by the light, only to crash fruitlessly again and again and again. Her desperation increased with each attempt to put it in the bag, but she would not kill a living thing trapped like herself in this airless fetid coffin. Yet she couldn't stand the sound, not one single minute longer. The stool was no good, she needed that to stand on. Her shoe would serve. It was heavy enough. Gathering the last shreds of her strength, she hammered with all her might at the barred window, not caring about the punishment to follow. It was tougher than she expected, but she would not give in. One more blow . . . another . . . With a sharp crack and the tinkle of falling glass, the bee winged away into freedom.

They were coming. The sound of footsteps mingled with the rattle of keys and opening doors. Voices echoed along the landing. Curses. Someone cried: 'Have pity!' In bed, Emily covered her head with the blanket. Shrieks now, and a single high-pitched scream of an animal in terror. A human animal. How was she to stand it? Perhaps it was only part of the nightmares that troubled sleep and spread out into the endless days. If only Louise was here. The touch of her hand. A warming, strengthening smile. But the last of Louise had been that hurried kiss before they were separated in the Bow Street cells.

'Number 13!'

It was no dream. The doctor speaking to her was the one who had examined her when she first entered Holloway.

'Listen carefully to what I have to say. Food has been brought for you and I give you a last chance to take it of your own free will.' He beckoned to a wardress standing behind.

Emily saw the glass of water and bowl of thin milky gruel. Everything else receded. Her thirst was a huge all-embracing drive. She shut her eyes tight, gripping the bedclothes.

'Very well. I have no other course than to compel you to take food.'

Her eyes still tightly closed, Emily felt the bedding stripped off and she was roughly pulled to her feet. A chair had been brought into the cell and she was made to sit down.

'Open your eyes, 13.'

He was holding a long tube made from two lengths of rubber joined by a glass junction. 'You still have a choice. This must pass into your stomach. It is easier by mouth.'

Emily clenched her teeth.

'Very well!' He signalled to the group of wardresses. Two came and held her shoulders, two more leaned on her legs, another grasped her head. As the doctor approached, Emily saw hairs sprouting from his nose, and the large pores of his skin. Then there was nothing but the agony of the tube being forced up her nostril.

In spite of herself she yelled out; begging for mercy, but there was no escape. The tube pressed down her throat into her stomach with a burning tearing sensation that stretched to the end of her breastbone. She stared up with wide anguished eyes and saw the doctor raise the funnel end and pour a brownish liquid into it.

She must suffocate! Her distended stomach heaved. Pain tore throat and nose, searing tender membrane. There was thunder in her head and a waterfall in her ears. No more . . . no more . . . no more . . . But the pain increased in ferocity as the tube was withdrawn, as if a hand were wrenching out the back of her nose and throat. Her body in revolt, she retched, spraying herself and her captors with vomit.

14

It was a fine day when Emily was released from Holloway. She blinked coming out into the clear sunlight.

'Goodbye then,' said the prison officer. 'If you take my advice you'll give up all that Suffragette nonsense. That's if you don't want another stretch.'

Emily did not reply and barely nodded. The door closed and the heavy key turned. The whole degrading episode lay behind her now. She did not want to talk or think about it any more. But was that possible? How was she to live with her conscience? She had failed; given in to her weak body; accepted food because the horror of being forcibly fed again was more than she could bear. The shame of it was something she must learn to live with. It had been terrible enough alone in her cell, but now she had to face Louise and Vera and all the other noble heroic souls who had stuck it out. She hated herself.

The sunshine was so bright and there were carts and omnibuses bowling along the road. People hurried past, smiling and talking. Free! Above, small clouds dappled the sky and as she looked up a pigeon wheeled, sailing down to land a few yards away. In the long six weeks she had almost forgotten how blue sky could be and the bright fresh green of new leaves. Her spirits took an upward step. She'd failed, but that didn't mean to say she couldn't pick up the shattered pieces and try to make something of them. She straightened her back . . . and saw the Maudslay, Peter standing in front. Panic set in and she half turned, meaning to hammer on the prison gate and beg to be taken back. Anything rather than face Peter.

'Emily! This is marvellous. I'm glad to see you.'

There was no escape.

'Hello, Peter.' Her voice was husky, and she dared not look directly at him.

He took her hand in both of his, shaking it again and again as if he would never let go. 'So pleased . . . so pleased . . .' he was saying.

She managed a shaky smile, knowing that the questions about Louise and Vera should be tumbling out, but unable to say a word.

'There's someone else waiting to see you,' Peter said, still holding her hand, leading her towards the car. 'There was to be a deputation as well. Mary Grant wanted to organize one with a special meal to celebrate your release, but I dissuaded her.' He looked as if he was trying to guess her reaction, then went on hurriedly: 'Too much risk really, the police being so hot on the trail of anyone connected with the Suffragettes – besides, May and I wanted you to ourselves.'

May! There she was, struggling to lower herself from the car. Emily pulled away from Peter and ran, gathering her into a hug that almost squeezed the breath out of her body. May was crying and laughing all at the same time.

'Oh, Emmie, I thought you was never going to get out. It seemed like ten thousand years. But it don't matter now because yo're here.' She began kissing Emily's cheeks, wetting them with her tears and pushing her hat askew, words wriggling out between the kisses. 'Mrs Silver's got a lovely breakfast waiting for yo . . . and I've had a letter from Mam . . . the new baby's called Edith *Emmeline*, what do yo think of that? And Dad's back at work . . . with Mr Treedle, delivering beer barrels . . . he's boss of the dray and the horse is called Sweetheart . . .'

'Hold hard,' Peter said. 'You'll leave no news for me to tell and Mrs Silver's kippers will have dried up.'

'Oh, kippers!' Emily said and burst into tears.

'Don't yo like them any more?' May asked in dismay. 'I told her they were your favourite.'

Emily struggled for control. 'It's not that, lovie, it's . . .' but she couldn't explain even to herself.

She sat in the back of the car with May, so there was no chance of conversation with Peter. It was a relief. She could cope with May's prattle, but was not ready for perceptive questioning. She'd have to be ready by the end of the ride. Were the answers to be found amongst the sweating horses, the cabbies with their bowler hats rakish, back-of-the-head, the flower women, the bustling shoppers streaming past her window?

'I've a present for you,' May said diffidently.

'What is it?'

'Secret, till we gets back.'

There were secrets everywhere, with not a word mentioned about Vera or Louise. It was her place to discover these secrets, but the obstacle of her own shame seemed too great to clamber over. Wait till they reached their destination. A brief question on the doorstep would cover her duty to Peter, though it was no consolation when she longed to know every last detail of Louise's prison experience. She had been released within a week. The prison grapevine had furnished that much information. Vera had been admitted to the prison hospital; afterwards her progress was shrouded in mystery. Don't think too deep. Not yet . . .

Mrs Silver was on the doorstep smiling a welcome fit for a hero, which made Emily feel worse than ever. Peter opened the door of the car, bowing as if for royalty. With her insides shrivelling, Emily crept on to the pavement.

'I'm ever so grateful . . .' she began.

'It's us who ought to be grateful,' Peter interrupted, and when she looked at him blankly, added: 'For the privilege of being able to help, even in a small way.'

Although she felt like an unwholesome cockroach Emily couldn't help asking: 'Yo mean that?'

'Of course.'

'But I thought yo thought us loonies.'

'I do. Stark raving mad, the lot of you. The world keeps producing such crazy fools, and often they do a lot of good.'

Emily was astounded, and if Mrs Silver hadn't taken her hand, drawing her into the house, she would have gone on staring stupidly at him.

'Mr Marshall too,' Mrs Silver beckoned. 'Your sister would never forgive me if I let you slip away.'

'Louise here?' Emily was thrilled and horrified.

Peter was helping May into the cramped hallway. 'Go in the parlour,' May called, and to Peter: 'I'll manage now.'

Coals of fire! Emily took off her hat, hurriedly trying to rake the pitiful ashes of her courage together. Well, she'd ached for some kind of scourge, hadn't she? This was it!

The parlour table was spread with a white damask cloth, sparkling silver and the best Crown Derby china. Little cottage loaves were piled in a dish at one end; sugar, cream and milk at the other; in the middle, a mass of yellow daffodils in a glass vase. A fragrant aroma of coffee filled the air.

'Welcome back to civilization,' Louise said, getting up from an armchair and coming to kiss her.

'How are you, Emily?' Miss Feather was hovering in the background, while Mrs Silver trotted backwards and forwards rearranging the flowers, straightening the cutlery and refolding napkins.

She loved them all. They were kind. So anxious to make her feel warm and wanted. Perhaps they didn't know? But they must do. She'd served the full six weeks of her sentence. Nobody could starve that long. Louise had been out in a week. And Vera? She was there on the sofa, thinner than ever. Her face like wax with a faint bluish tinge round her mouth. Emily knelt by her. There was so much and nothing to say.

'Hello, Emmie,' Vera said in a voice fragile as cobwebs.

Emily took one bird's claw and held it close to her cheek. 'Yo all right then?' Such meaningless words. One look was enough to tell that Vera was far from all right.

'Bit dicky, but they've not killed me yet.' She began coughing; a grinding cough that went on and on. Fine sweat stood on her forehead and her shoulders hunched with effort. When the spasm was over she lay back against the cushions, eyes closed, apparently exhausted.

Emily was alarmed. 'How long has she been like this?' she asked Mrs Silver.

'Since she left the prison hospital.'

Vera opened her eyes. 'Get started,' she said. 'I want me kipper.'

They gathered round the table with a great deal of chatter and forced laughter, but before they could begin the meal, May came hobbling in from the hall.

'Wait a minute. She ain't had the present yet.' She was holding a brown paper packet.

Emily took it, untying the string. Inside was a tapestry purse with a metal clasp and long chain handle. On the front, worked in purple, green and white was the badge of the W.S.P.U.

'Go on . . . open it!'

A screw of tissue paper was tucked into a pocket with a card. She read – 'To Emily Palmer. With grateful thanks for your courage and devotion – Emmeline Pankhurst.' The tissue paper held a silver brooch in the shape of a portcullis with a broken chain hanging either side, and a medallion which had been inscribed HUNGER STRIKE.

'I made the purse,' May said.

If she had been overcome before, she was now demolished. There were no words that could tell them her feelings because she didn't understand them herself.

'Speech . . . speech . . .'

She saw them through a mist of tears. The effort of saying: 'Speeches ain't my line,' was enormous, but the discipline was all she had to offer. She went on: 'Thanks ever so much. Yo don't know . . . what a fraud I am. I don't deserve any of this.' She blinked back the tears and took a deep breath. 'But I'll do better next time, see if I don't.'

There was some clapping and she sat down conscious of being red and sweaty with effort, but also a little easier in her mind.

'Taste that!' Louise was ecstatic, her mouth full of kipper. 'Puts the old prison gruel and brown rock into the category of pig swill.'

The comment rubbed over Emily's sore mind like sandpaper. Answering lightheartedly was part of the ordeal.

'Worse! Pig swill smells quite savoury.'

'Have another,' Mrs Silver said, coming round with the dish. 'Vera, you've not touched yours yet. Won't build up your strength that way.'

'I'm sorry,' Vera said faintly. 'Can't seem to manage. In a minute, perhaps.'

Sitting beside Emily, Peter leaned across her to ask Louise in a low voice: 'Has she seen a doctor? She's in a bad way.'

Emily was supremely conscious of him. He smelled freshly masculine and the sandy hair curled behind his ears which were pink and scrubbed. Prison had not damped down her ridiculous emotions, indeed they seemed intensified.

'He's been more than once,' Louise answered.

'What does he say?'

'It's difficult . . . here.' Louise said. She gave a tiny shrug and with one swift blow as she soundlessly framed the word 'heart', cancelled Emily's sentimental doting.

'Let me help get the coffee,' Emily said, getting up and following Mrs Silver into the kitchen. She had to know. 'Is it bad, Vera's heart trouble?'

'Bad enough.' Mrs Silver handed her the coffee-pot. 'I didn't want to talk about it at the celebration really. It's complicated by her bronchitis. One sets the other going. Sort of vicious circle. And the three times those devils force fed her made matters worse.'

'Oh God!'

'She's bound to be an invalid always, Dr Curtis says.'

'But what'll she do? She's got no family I knows of.'

'Don't you worry on that score. Miss Marshall has already promised her a home in return for a little light sewing, so as she doesn't feel it's charity. Not that I'd turn her out, but I've a business to run.' She began dabbing teaspoons into a row of cups and saucers. 'That Liberal Government's got a lot to answer for. There's that poor Emily Wilding Davison dead, killed by the King's horse at the Derby and Mrs Pankhurst's sister gone too. Where'll it end, that's what I'd like to know?'

Where indeed? Carrying the coffee-pot back into the parlour, Emily felt more deeply ashamed than ever.

Shame became a constant companion over the following weeks. It was with her now as she sat by Vera's bed in the little back room Mrs Silver had given her for privacy. She squeezed out the sponge and wiped Vera's feverish face.

'You've got nice hands.' Vera's voice was breathy.

'What, my great lumps of meat?'

'Capable.'

She was silent for a while and Emily tried to busy herself with the piece of tucking she had brought to do during the long night hours. The soft pearly light, cast by an oil lamp standing on the table beside her, encouraged sleep more than anything else. She stifled a yawn. On the mantelpiece the clock said half past two. Three more hours before Mrs Silver took over, and then there would be a couple of blessed hours for sleep before tackling the work of the day. It couldn't go on like this. They'd have to get a nurse to come and help. If only the doctor would let her be moved, then she could go back to Birmingham and live at the Tower House. Louise had returned to prison. No starving this time. She intended completing her sentence, feeling responsible for Vera, as much as Emily did.

'Emmie?'

'What?'

'There's something I've been thinking I ought to tell you. It's about Vic. I'm . . . was very fond of him. P'raps you wouldn't know, the way I treated him. He wanted me to . . . marry him . . . but I said no. Couldn't. You must tell him . . .' Her words disappeared into a bout of coughing which left her limp and ashen. 'It was because of . . .' She struggled for breath.

'Don't talk now. It'll keep till yo're stronger,' Emily urged.

Vera shook her head. 'My baby,' she whispered.

'*Your* baby?' In spite of herself Emily couldn't keep the astonishment out of her voice. 'But I never knew . . .'

And then she did in a flash. It was the reason Vera had left domestic service and her hopes of becoming cook; why she had always been so shut in on herself; why more than anything she had been so frosty with Vic.

'Dora I called her. She only lived three weeks. The master of the house I worked at in London was her father. So now you know it. You can tell Vic.'

'Why don't yo tell him? He'll stand by yo. I'll write and ask him to come on his next leave, then yo can have a real heart to heart and straighten things out. It'll be easy as anything, yo see!' It was a relief to say something cheerful and constructive.

'Don't let's pretend, Emmie,' Vera said.

'I'm not pretending. Yo'd do fine as my sister.'

Vera felt for her hand. Taking it, Emily was almost afraid she might crush the brittle bones.

'We've all got to die,' Vera said. 'Really I don't mind. Living can be . . . too difficult.'

Emily sat holding her hand. Silent. In the face of death, pretence became an insult.

15

A DEPUTATION to the King! Surely that must bring results?

'Will you come?' Mary Grant asked.

Emily still hesitated. In theory she approved, but to take part was an entirely different matter. Vera's death two weeks ago had destroyed an inner conviction. Taken the heart out of her. She had resigned from the Bodyguard and gone to no more meetings.

'Louise can't come for obvious reasons, unless she gets remission, and that's hardly likely!'

It would be walking straight into the jaws of the enemy. How far would they get before the inevitable battle began?

'Are you afraid?' The question was gentle enough, but Emily reacted strongly.

'No, of course I ain't. I'm just not . . . convinced any more.'

The expression of Mary's face was one of total disbelief into which crept a flicker of doubt. 'You aren't trying to tell me that you no longer care whether we achieve the right to vote? A person of your intelligence can't possibly . . .'

'No, it isn't that,' Emily interrupted. She shrugged to find the right words to make hard fact out of her intangible feelings. 'All the violence . . . where's it getting us?'

'Nearer our goal.'

'With folk turning against us because of it and people dying for nothing? I've heard some of the bastards say we deserve to die — "Let 'em get on with it" — when we starve in prison.' The shame connected with hunger striking covered her like a hair shirt, but she had steeled herself to mentioning it when the need was there.

Mary looked at her with compassion. 'If you are thinking of Vera . . .'

'Course I'm thinking of her. I think of her all the time.

It's such a *waste*! She'd only got one life . . . we all have, and to throw it away . . .'

Emily got up and went to the parlour window, staring angrily into the cramped Soho street. Shame and anger and disillusion – she didn't know which she felt most.

'Vera gave her life willingly, for the Cause. Just as I would, or Louise, or any of us if it had to be that way.'

It's not true, Emily thought. Things snowballed for Vera. She got involved almost against her will.

Mary got up, collecting her gloves and smoothing her dress preparatory to leaving. 'I won't press you, Emily. Everyone has to follow the dictates of their conscience. I'm disappointed naturally, especially as Louise is in prison. I'd thought you would like to step in for her, even if you don't want to join the ranks of the Bodyguard.'

Impulsively Emily turned round, all her doubts gone in a rush of affection for Louise. 'I'll come,' she said. What were scruples compared with love!

'Oh!' Mary was disconcerted, then she smiled. 'I'm glad. Now I'd better tell you the arrangements. It's planned for the twenty-first of May. We've organized a house in Grosvenor Place. It's at the back of Buckingham Palace, overlooking the gardens. Of course we shall have to be very careful not to make the police suspicious so the idea is to arrive in ones and twos over a period of days. It'll be a question of camping out, I'm afraid.'

'That won't worry me; I've slept on the floor when my bed's been in hock before now!'

'There will be some sort of sleeping and eating arrangements, don't worry. Then, on the day, we will set out to walk up Constitution Hill to the gates of the Palace and try to gain entrance to deliver the Petition. Mrs Pankhurst will lead us and we shall be in groups of ten, each with a captain, vice-captain and so on. The idea being if there is trouble and people get arrested, there will always be another to carry on.'

Emily saw her to the door and waved goodbye. In her bones she felt the scheme was bound for failure. And yet it was the right of every Englishman or woman to take their grievances to their King. If it was finally denied it would be a body-blow. In all fairness he must listen. And if there was any justice at all he would surely come down on their side? But even as she closed the door, misgivings were already cooling her impetuous emotions.

Emily felt no better as she approached the house in Grosvenor Place. Four storeys of highly respectable opulence with stone steps leading up to an imposing porch and solid panelled door. Having decided on the role of seamstress delivering some garment, it had seemed sensible to arrive on the actual day. So now, with a large striped dress-box tucked under one arm, she went discreetly down the area steps and knocked at the tradesmen's door.

'Emily Palmer,' introducing herself to a round little woman in black with a red nose and haystack hair.

'Oh come in ... come in ... it's a regular party. Mary Grant was just talking about you. We thought you weren't going to manage to get here in time. Elsie's making a last cup of tea before we set out.'

Elsie, sleeves rolled to the elbow and face sweating faintly with effort, was lifting a large black kettle from a gas ring to pour a stream of boiling water into a brown enamel teapot. She looked up with a smile and told Emily to help herself to a mug and then tell the other ladies to come.

The interior of the house was an extraordinary contrast to the outside, like stepping into a makeshift stage set. Empty of furniture, it was filled with women. They were everywhere, in the hall, on the stairs, inside each room, putting on hats and coats, drinking tea, chatting with occasional bursts of laughter. Emily felt an air of barely controlled excitement that was at the same time stimulating and uncomfortable. She said as much to Mary Grant in a brief lull between her bouts of organizing.

'Nerve-racking,' Mary agreed, skewering her hat on to puffs of hair with a dangerous-looking hatpin. 'I've got the most awful butterflies.'

'I wish Louise was here.'

'She is in spirit.'

And a fat lot of good that is, was Emily's last inward-looking thought because final instructions were being given and banners unfolded. She found she was to be in a group with Mary as captain. The other eight were familiar faces from meetings she had attended. A girl close by, holding one end of a banner, turned to Emily.

'Here, catch hold of this a minute will you, while I give me stays a tug. Must have laced 'em too tight . . . they're giving me what for. Not seen you around for a while. Been doing time?'

'Not recently.'

'Didn't think to see you here, darlin'.' Emily felt an arm round her shoulder and saw her friend from bodyguard days who had been tried at Bow Street with her. 'You brought your clubs?'

Emily shook her head. 'I resigned, remember? I'll just walk along.'

'Well if there's trouble, I know you won't be backward in coming forward!' She leaned close, adding confidentially: 'We've a trick up our sleeves to keep any troublemakers at bay – look at this!' She produced two paper bags. 'Pepper. Assorted colours to make it more interesting . . . green and red. It'll tickle a few noses!' She nudged Emily's ribs. 'I must be off. Mrs Pankhurst's ready and we've to get into rank.'

Emily came out into the hall and saw Emmeline Pankhurst in front of the Bodyguard. A small elegant figure in dark well-cut clothes, her face worn with the rigours of innumerable hunger strikes. But there was something indomitable about her. Was it the authoritative straightness of her spine or the fine bone structure and piercing eyes that eclipsed lines and taut hollows? Emily could not be sure, but she was conscious of a beauty that merged into a hypnotice magic with the minor cadences of her voice as she spoke last-minute words of encouragement.

Walking along Grosvenor Place towards Constitution Hill, the feelings those words had inspired in Emily began to diminish. She looked up at the back wall of the Palace gardens. It seemed to represent all the obstacles standing between Women and the coveted Vote, and looked just as impossible to scale. In the open air of this pale sunlit afternoon there was a nakedness about the venture that was not helped by her growing conviction it was doomed to failure. A light breeze brushed her cheeks and pushed against the banner which she had offered to share carrying. At the head of the small column was Mrs Pankhurst, flanked by the Bodyguard. Seeing them, Emily felt a twinge of conscience as though she was playing traitor for a second time.

Oh give over, she told herself, thinking's all very well ... it's what happens in the next half-hour that counts.

And the next half-hour was already promising to be lively. From a quiet unobtrusive procession, they were becoming objects of curiosity. Passers-by were gazing at them as if they had come from Mars, and ahead, by the Wellington Gates, was a crowd. Some were sympathizers waiting to join the demonstration, but there were also an ominous number of police, mounted and on foot.

A murmur spread backwards, thrown from shoulder to shoulder: 'The Gates ... they are shutting the Wellington Gates ... we'll never get through!'

Closing round were the inevitable knots of jeering young men in high collars and bowler hats, umbrellas at the ready to prod as they shouted the usual taunts. 'Get back to your husbands ... their kids'll go hungry today ... lot of old crows ...'

They were almost there. Looking between iron railings, Emily saw the wide tree-lined road that was Constitution Hill, empty now except for a police cordon and a few protected bystanders. It was like looking into the free world from behind prison bars. The main gates were already closed and locked. No use bothering with those, but one of the side gates had not yet been fastened. Already some of the women were climbing on the railings, pushing and shoving, struggling to get through. Indian clubs whirled among the encroaching mob. From being a well-ordered procession they were divided into small groups. Elbowing with all her might, Emily pushed forward, helped by the pressure of bodies from behind. One of the police horses was edging towards her, its great piebald haunches moving sideways, the rider shouting:

'Closed! No way through.'

What had happened to Mrs Pankhurst? Ogling sight-seers, cheek by jowl with those familiar blue uniforms that made Emily's stomach turn over, cut off any view. She must get there . . . she must . . . With a final tremendous thrust, she squeezed close to the railings, but the side gate was shut. Beyond was the astonishing sight of Mrs Pankhurst with some of her Bodyguard hurrying in the direction of the Palace. For Emily it was a triumph and a personal failure. But she was given no time to dwell on her feelings.

'Get a hold of her, Jack . . . throw her this way.'

She felt her collar grabbed and was flung towards her tormentor, but not before she had jabbed an elbow with some force into the unseen Jack's stomach. She heard him grunt and was saved from the blow aimed at her by being shoved headlong into a mass of heaving bodies. There was no time for thought. All principles about no violence were lost in a desperate need for self-preservation. Handbags, truncheons and clubs met flesh in agonizing blows. One crunched on her shoulder, sending tingling pain to her fingertips. She felt her voice shout obscenities that were lost in the yells and screams buffeting her ears. There was anger in her now, a bursting fury that needed expression, but crushed as she was against the lathering flank of a police horse it was all she could do to prevent herself from being trampled underfoot. She glimpsed a hat skim-ming the air. The horse flicked its tail and as it danced sideways, a woman, armed with a pair of secateurs, cut through the bridle. The rider swore, kicking out as he dismounted and scoring Emily's cheek. The pain dug through her head and, hand to face, she was distantly surprised to feel blood oozing between her fingers. She felt none of the fear she had experienced in prison. All the injustice in the world, the savage prison cruelties, the innocent deaths, seemed concentrated in this battle. Boiling with it, Emily strained to raise her elbows enough to lam them backwards, momentarily clearing a space showing her that the mob was not entirely hostile. There were men fighting men, others with protective arms round dazed women.

'That's it, comrades – show the bastards . . .' she bawled as the gap closed and the crowd shifted, knocking her off her feet. She did not fall. Tight-packed bodies pinioned her arms, wringing the breath from her lungs. Her hat had gone and her hair tumbled free. Another shift. Fists punched. A horse neighed above the howls of the mob and helplessly Emily was sucked down into a sea of bodies which closed over her head. Her courage died as light was shut out. Sheer panic doubled her strength, but several hundredweight of flesh and bone pressed her relentlessly down. In the jungle of trouser legs, torn skirts and thudding boots there was no escape and her shouts for help were choked in tweed and flannel. Trodden and kicked, her hair hooked on buttons and torn from her head, she would have been lost if the tide of movement had not changed. There were shouts of: 'Someone's down . . . look out for the woman . . . mind yer feet,' as a policeman guided his horse to divide the crowd.

Hazy with pain, Emily opened her eyes to a patch of primrose sky. There were elbows and knees knitting and unravelling against it. Must get out . . . get out . . . Pain buckled her limbs and sapped her strength. The effort to push up into that living space was beyond her . . . but she was doing it. Not alone. A line of pressure across her spine meant someone was lifting. She thought she saw Peter before the oncoming horse wedged between them. A miracle if it was. And then the support was gone, dragged away, and she slithered down a hill of bodies to be shot into instant darkness with a single glancing flick of the horse's hoof.

16

THE primrose sky had gone. All she could smell was carbolic edged with lavender. Alone, in bed . . . her bed. No, not quite alone, there were faces, May's, Mrs Silver's . . . both worried. Four cracks in the ceiling that she'd never noticed before. Below the picture rail a faded bunch of wallpaper cherries garnished with a solitary fly.

Emily shut her eyes tight.

'She's come to.' A scuffle of feet and the bed bounced.

Emily opened her eyes and looked at Peter. She was vaguely surprised, but there didn't seem much logic about anything at that moment.

'Emily?'

The sound of his voice warmed her. The glow started in the pit of her stomach and began spreading through her body like brandy. Another face now. Older, with a sharp white beard and ferocious eyebrows. Dr Curtis.

'What's wrong with me?' she said in a loud firm voice that came out a weak whisper.

He was taking her pulse, the other hand on her head where the dull ache sat.

'Nothing that a bit of rest and care won't cure,' Dr Curtis said. 'You had a nasty knock on the head. Don't you remember?'

She began to shake her head, but a razor of pain sliced through her skull.

'A horse kicked yo . . . by the Wellington Gates, when yo was with the Suffragettes. Mr Marshall brought yo home.' May was hanging on to the bedpost, looking down with an anxious smile, waiting to be reassured.

'Ssh . . . she'll remember all in good time. Don't worry her now . . .'

They were going away. Dr Curtis talking in undertones. The sound of May hobbling over the lino. It was all wrong. She didn't want to be alone. And Peter?

He came over to the bed to say goodbye.

'Stay . . . please.' She pulled a strangely heavy hand from under the starched sheet and when he took it her relief was complete.

'Just for a bit, then,' he said. 'The doctor says you need quiet, so we won't talk.'

That was all right. She didn't want conversation, just contact. She'd never been a great one for words anyway. Sometimes talking was a nuisance.

A fly buzzed overhead, circling down to land on the washstand. She watched it trek round the lip of the water-jug. For a moment she was safe.

When she woke again twilight had crawled into the room. The cheerful clatter from the street seemed locked out and she was lying in a pool of silence that chilled in spite of the warm air. The pain in her head had receded and she raised herself from the pillows, desperate for company. No one was there. She wanted to cry out, but a thin patch of common sense prevented her and she flopped back. There was nothing now to stop the march of her thoughts. Emily Palmer, seamstress from the back-streets of Brum, thrown by chance into an exciting whirl-pool of promise about fresh horizons with people whose incisive minds cut new patterns in her emotions. The truth was she had allowed herself to dream along with them, even fall in love with them. Louise and Peter! They merged, then separated. Golden people; the stuff of dreams. And all that about freedom! Freedom for what? To burn houses and break windows, get thumped and tortured? From a cloud-topped castle in the air she was back in the dust. If only Peter were still with her, but he wasn't and never likely to be.

'Face it, Emily, it's a life of toil for yo . . . just like Mam and May and all them other working women . . . unless yo wants to starve or go on the streets.'

She rolled over, burying her tender face in the pillow, too weary even for the relief of tears.

A bunch of black grapes and a posy of sweet-william wrapped in a silver-lace doily. There was a note tied with red ribbon. 'To cheer you up – from Louise and Peter.'

'D'yo think they knew it's your birthday?' May asked.

'Don't suppose so. It's just a coincidence.' Emily ate one of the grapes then pushed them across the sewing table. 'Go on, help yourselves.'

'Get along with you! They were sent specially for the invalid,' Mrs Silver said, sticking pins at a furious rate into scarlet taffeta.

'I'm *not* an invalid,' Emily assured her.

'Up and doing far too soon.'

'Yo are one hand short as it is and with me lying in bed yo'd never manage. Besides I felt like a real cheat up there, lolling about like some frail little waif. Me with my muscles!' She spoke with forced cheerfulness. The oblique reference to Vera had capped her regular mood of stale flatness which alternated with a deep panicky shame about the way she had abandoned the Suffragettes. She tried to write it off as depression resulting from four weeks in bed because of her injuries, but had to admit she had been slipping downhill before then.

'Pity our Vic ain't coming after all,' May said.

Privately Emily had been very relieved to get his short letter saying he had decided to go back to Birmingham for his week's leave so he could meet Edith Emmeline. Afterwards he was being posted to some unknown place. There was a strong rumour of war and he was glad. After all, what were soldiers for? He wants to get killed, Emily had thought and then told herself not to be so gloomy.

She ate another grape, went to put the flowers in a jam jar and came back to the skirt she was seaming. The thick cloth felt particularly heavy. She stopped treadling the machine, unaware she was being watched, and slipped into a muddle of thoughts that just would not resolve themselves. It would be so easy if things stayed black and white, but they were far too complicated. She sighed.

'I've been thinking we ought to have a tot of gin to celebrate, then take a half-holiday.' Mrs Silver looked at Emily speculatively.

'What, with all this work?' Emily was astonished.

'You take May to see Miss Marshall. She's been on at

you to visit for a long while. A breath of fresh air'll do you the world of good. And you can deliver that blouse to Mrs Boston if it'll make you feel any better,' cutting across Emily's protests. 'Get the gin now, there's a good girl. Glasses are in the top of the dresser.' And Mrs Silver filled her mouth with pins.

There was a hot breath of summer pushing into the chintz sitting-room at Holland Park. Through open windows drifted a sweetness of roses and the drowsy hum of bees. Coming in, Emily saw scattered books and magazines, coat and gloves carelessly flung over the back of a chair, and exchanged the picture for a photograph in her mind of the last visit. They were almost identical. Only the table beneath the oval mirror was different; empty; the hat long disappeared. Louise had changed too. Looking at her grey face and emaciated body, Emily wanted to swear. She had been right. Violence got you nothing but pain.

Louise put down the newspaper with a cry of pleasure. 'This is splendid . . . much better than reading about those absurd Croats and Serbians playing cloak-and-dagger games. Come and sit down. May too . . . and a parcel! It's like Christmas.'

'Birthday,' May said.

'Yours?'

'No, mine.' Emily put down the dress-box. 'I've brought Mrs Boston's blouse. And thanks for the grapes and flowers.'

'They came today? How clever of Peter to know.'

'Was it his idea?' Emily could feel the blush working through her body.

'Combined really, though how he managed to find out about your birthday is a mystery.'

'Accident I expect.'

'Whatever it was, things worked out right. Now come and sit down . . . move the leaflets will you? As a matter of fact I wanted to ask you about those. I need people to distribute them . . . for the Cause.' She looked hard at Emily. 'Not willing?'

What was she to say? There was such a muddle in her

mind. Frayed ends of ideas. Reluctance.

Louise tapped the pile of paper. 'I'd do it myself, only my legs misbehave when I stand up.'

And guilt. Hypocrisy to go on doing easy things like giving out leaflets when she'd betrayed her friends by shying from torture in prison. Why was she plagued with the feeling that it should be all or nothing? She couldn't face *all*. And violence was wrong. Suffragettes were violence.

May chipped in with: 'Let me take them leaflets round. When I've my sticks to lean on I can manage nicely and I've wanted to help for ages.'

The offer was more than Emily could bear. The old bogey of speechlessness was haunting her, but she knew she must say something. The words, when they came were all wrong and her voice cracked.

'I feel that bad.'

Louise looked worried. 'Here, sit down – you do look washed out. Are you feeling faint?'

Emily shook her head. 'It ain't that, it's what I did. Yo must know . . . news travels well enough in prison . . . I . . .' She swallowed, the words almost drying on her tongue. With a great effort she pushed them out: 'I ain't brave like yo. I never took more than the one forced feeding.'

She looked away, shame weighing on her, not wanting to see the scorn in Louise's eyes.

'And you've been nursing these guilty feelings all this time without a word to anyone . . . you old silly!' Louise spoke gently and Emily felt the pressure of her hand. She dared to look up and found Louise smiling.

'Yo ain't disgusted?'

Louise didn't answer directly. 'Who has taken any number of beatings and overridden the fear of public speaking? You may think of yourself as a coward . . . no one else does.'

'That ain't all though. I can't believe it's right.'

'What – Votes for Women?' Louise sounded startled.

'Oh I believe in that, but not the way we does it. The violence; it's all wrong . . . it don't seem the way to get what we're after. I just don't know — I'm not sure what to do any more.'

'Do whatever your conscience tells you, of course,' Louise said firmly. 'There isn't one way only. If peaceful protests are right for you, then that is your path. But don't ever feel alone, not for one minute. There are hordes of us, massed together, all with the same goal, all comrades, and that is our strength.'

Echoes from so many stirring speeches touched Emily's mind, creating a ripple of new conviction, yet her vision of the violence as useless and degrading remained; pricking doubts which she could not escape. For the moment Louise's warm response made the guilty shadows of the past weeks fade, bringing a great lifting relief. She squeezed Louise's hand hard, near to tears, which, if the sound of muffled voices in the hall hadn't intruded, would have spilled over.

A door banged and footsteps came closer.

'What a journey . . . you wouldn't believe! Two punctures, the electrical circuit failed and I got tangled with four herds of cattle, not to mention an escaped pig!' Peter burst into the room with a draught of air that set the curtains billowing. For a fraction of a moment Emily thought she saw more than surprise in his expression as their eyes met. Then it was gone and he was smiling in a friendly way. 'Emily! I'd no idea you would be here . . . Lou, you never said!' He wrapped Louise in a bear-hug, looking all the while at Emily.

'I didn't know she was going to call. I was just as surprised as you,' Louise said, coming up for air.

Peter released her and came to Emily, putting a hand on her arm. 'Are you better now? I would have visited again, but I've been in Birmingham. Since Father died, my time's not my own.'

'Y . . . yes . . . I'm well enough.' She was bounced from one kind of emotional upheaval into another, relief giving way to humiliation. She felt as if he were looking right into her mind without giving her a chance to hide away her tender feelings.

'She ain't telling the truth,' May said. 'She's working

again when she should be resting. Mrs Silver goes on at her, but she don't take no notice.'

'Shut up, May!' and to Peter: 'Don't listen to her.'

'And I've been pressing you to deliver these leaflets. You should have said,' Louise chided.

Peter looked down at her. 'You must take care. Concussion can be a nasty thing.'

'I'm perfectly all right,' Emily protested fiercely. Lies! She was suffering like hell; not from a kick in the head, but this infatuation with him – intense, unpredictable, quite out of control. A silliness exposed for all to see. Why didn't he go and sit down somewhere? The bigness of him made her feel small and delicate. Her! And now she'd tied knots in the air by snapping. They were all staring. Oh sod everything!

'We can't stay long,' she said desperately.

'But you've time for some tea. I insist. I'm dying of thirst myself.' Peter rang for the maid. 'If you are late, I can always drive you back.'

'Don't bother.' Emily was ungracious with embarrassment.

'No bother. I'm free of work for the time being. In fact I was thinking of planning a balloon trip the weekend after next. Been promising myself the luxury for weeks. This is my first opportunity. You wouldn't like to come too?'

'Oo, Emmie!' No envy in May's eyes, only joy for her.

'Peter, you ought to let her see what she'd be letting herself in for first,' Louise said.

Peter tweaked her ear. 'Just because you are a ninny when it comes to heights, doesn't mean all women are the same. Emily's the pioneering type, aren't you?'

She had to say: 'I'll try anything once.' A truth that covered a wasp's nest of failure.

'Told you, didn't I!' he said triumphantly to Louise. 'It'll be a last fling.'

Louise frowned. 'What do you mean?'

'When the war starts we shan't be able to fly balloons . . . might drift across the channel. Besides, I'll be busy.'

'War . . . what war? You don't mean to tell me you

believe all that stuff in the papers.'

'Of course I do. It's not only unrest in Serbia. Austria is in trouble and England must stand by her friends.'

'Oh Peter . . . *really*!'

With a cold wind of winter chilling her bones, Emily remembered Vic's warning of a posting for active service. At least Peter wasn't a soldier.

A maid came in with the tea tray as he was saying: 'There's no point in scoffing, Lou.'

'Stop pacing about like an injured lion, have some tea and straighten out your screwed-up notions.' Louise was edgy, slopping tea as she poured.

Peter clicked his tongue irritably. He would have answered back, but as she watched, Emily saw his annoyed glance mellow. They were growing up. His compassion said as much. Looking at Louise, Emily felt the same compassion and it shunted head on into her hotchpotch of fear and guilt, clearing a passage. She knew what to do.

'Yo meant that . . . about going in a balloon?' she asked.

'Yes. Did you think I was fooling?'

She looked down at the floor, afraid of what he might read in her eyes. 'I just wanted to make sure.'

'And you'll come?'

'Yes!' The 'please' came a long way after.

17

SUNDAY was the proper day for church bells and dumplings
with stew and Dad getting secretly drunk. It had nothing
to do with going quite mad, climbing into a frail wickerwork basket suspended on bits of string and letting yourself be taken into the sky, helpless as a day-old mouse.
And yet that was just what she was about to do.

Emily stared at the long hose leading from a gas tap to
the mouth of a crumpled mass of green and white striped
silk that already was miraculously belling into balloon
shape.

'Our colours,' she said. 'Suffrage colours anyway.'

Peter smiled. 'Yes, a bit of organized luck there. Isn't
she a splendid sight? A real beauty!' He spoke with such
doting enthusiasm Emily felt as much jealousy as if he
were speaking about another woman. 'You won't mind if
I leave you for a bit? A good pilot always likes to check
everything is shipshape for himself. Come closer . . . so
you can see what goes on.'

Edging towards the hissing gas, Emily was astonished
that he couldn't sense either the love shining from her,
or her abysmal fear, or the trick she was going to play.
Anybody would think they were about to do nothing
more hair-raising than take a country walk!

A great deal of activity filled the grounds of the Aero
Club at Hurlingham. Three other balloons besides Peter's
were being prepared for flight. One was straining at the
mooring ropes, pushed about by a freshening wind.

'Good day for it,' Peter remarked on his way from one
side to the balloon to the other.

Bad day . . . a very bad day! Never had trees or grass
seemed so appealing or sane. Emily looked at her new
patent-leather shoes. There were roots growing through
the soles; she could feel them binding her to the soil. It
would be impossible for her to get into that imitation

laundry basket Peter kept referring to as 'the car'. She would tell him next time he passed. Then after he had flown away she could sneak back home, pick up her needle, stop meddling and put all her energy into practical things like earning her bread and seeing May right. It seemed an admirable and praiseworthy way out.

'Oh no yo won't, my gal,' she said aloud.

The man standing a couple of yards in front of her, turned round. 'What's that, miss?'

'Nothing . . . nothing at all.'

The balloon had filled with monstrous grace; threatening her. Peter was testing the ropes securing basket to balloon, adjusting the bags filled with sand for ballast and loading in the flight instruments, car rugs, hamper, cushions and a couple of folding stools. Nothing had been forgotten. Except my feelings, Emily thought. The balloon lurched with a sudden gust of wind and her stomach turned.

'She's raring to go,' called one of the men hanging on to the mooring ropes.

The first balloon had been released and the cheering surrounded Emily with no comfort at all. She watched it swaying and shrinking against a sky feathered with moving cloud.

'A fair wind, but that's all to the good.' Peter put a hand on her shoulder. Enough to melt her any other time, but now she was aware only of approaching doom. 'Ready?'

Doom had arrived. Grin and bear it!

'You are all right?'

'Me? Oh . . . yes!' The way she was feeling her face must be pea-green.

'Come on then and I'll help you in.'

Walking was difficult. Take it slow and stately. Careful or she'd lose everything, dignity included. A moment of alarm in case he suspected as he lifted her over the side of the car. The wickerwork creaked and shook as he scrambled in.

'You should take off your hat,' Peter said. 'Here, have this scarf to tie round your head.'

Obediently she passed her hat to Peter and wrapped

herself in his muffler. It smelled of wool soaked in his personal odour and was ridiculously warm for this fine first of July.

'All right then . . . we're ready.' Peter was pulling on the valve rope to let out excess gas. 'Hands off!'

Emily clutched the edge of the car. She dare not look up or down. There must be one spot of courage left to help her conquer the awful waves of panic! The unstable ground tilted, righting itself as the balloon shot into the air, steadied, then continued up more sedately.

God help me, what have I done, Emily was thinking as the ordinary world sank into waving hands, then tree-tops and chimney-stacks. A crow flew across the path of her fixed vision. Sky now, all round. Peter talking. A buzzing in her ears like bluebottles. And her guts threatening to drop out. In all her worst imaginings she had never expected to feel so shockingly frightened.

'Right now . . . trail rope fixed, grapnel in place, everything in order – next thing, admire the view. Emily? You've got your eyes shut!' He sounded accusing, then surprised: 'You aren't scared?'

'Bloody petrified!'

She felt his arm go round her shoulder and pull her close. A little courage seeped back along with a lot of other emotions that wound up her heart and set it careering round her ribs.

'Old goose!'

It wasn't what you'd call an endearment, but it would do for now. She opened her eyes a crack, coming out of the darkness of his rough tweed jacket, slewing round to take a peep over the edge of the basket.

'There now . . . it's not so bad, is it?'

'Why aren't we moving?' The buzzing had gone from her ears and the stillness surrounding them was broken only by the wind singing through the ropes. He began to laugh; the same well-remembered gusty sound that Louise made. Impossible not to join in even if you didn't know why.

'Look down!'

Hanging on for dear life, she craned over the chest-high wickerwork. Rolling below was a pageant of roof-tops and spires tied up with ribbon roads dotted with ants. It wasn't the balloon that was moving, it was the world; scenes ever shifting. Parks and people. Pincushion life. Horses and carts from a toyshop. Washing-line flags. The snaking Thames alive with barge sails and sunshine stars.

With the return of her senses Emily remembered her plan. And she was late! They were miles above London . . . hundreds of feet anyway. There was no time to be lost. But how in the world could she hitch up her skirt and petticoat in this square inch of space with Peter right next to her?

'I've got something for you,' Peter said, squatting in front of the hamper. He held out a leaflet.

She began to giggle. 'Yo too!'

'What do you mean?'

'Brought some of them Suffragette leaflets Louise had.' He stared at her with dawning understanding. 'Have you?'

She nodded.

'Where are they?'

'In my bloomers!' She snorted out laughter, seeing his face crinkle. 'But it's a bit awkward . . . getting at them.'

Peter doubled up, snatching at breath and words. Coming on top of all the other things swinging her about, they left her tipsy.

'You marvellous girl . . . one in a million!'

Her cheeks on fire, she said: 'If we're going to throw them over, we'd better get on with it.'

He got up, politely turning his back and she rooted under her skirt, showering leaflets round her feet.

'Yo can look now,' she said, shovelling them into a heap.

'You first.'

She took a fistful and let go. They fluttered and spread like great white butterflies, tumbling towards the rooftops.

'Now your turn.'

By a trick of the wind Peter's sheaf swirled backwards, flicking their faces before being carried out and down.

Emily laughed hysterically, excitement walling in her fear as she gathered more handfuls, flinging them out. Crazy July snow for the people trudging along everyday streets. She could imagine them staring and pointing. They would see the drifting balloon – a giant's toy – but not her fear, which was as real as the basket under her hand. She was still clammy with fright, but she'd conquered her shame!

'I've done it!' she shouted as the last white sheet fluttered way.

'A true Suffragette.'

She looked at him sharply, the compliment cut down by the tone of his voice.

'I'd hoped you might have come . . . for the fun of it.'

It was on the tip of her tongue to say 'I did', but she couldn't lie to him. The triumph in her dwindled.

'Wild horses wouldn't have dragged me, but I was . . . ashamed,' she said.

He frowned in a puzzled way.

She muttered: 'Not being able to stand it in prison. Betraying them . . . Louise . . . Mrs Pankhurst . . . all of them.' She could see he didn't understand. Words were the devil. 'I had to do something that took all my courage.'

'I see,' but he wasn't sure.

'Something that wasn't violent.'

He seemed to accept her explanation, but said nothing in return, turning to look at the flight instruments and busy himself with a routine check of the balloon. Emily sat down miserably on one of the cushions. Elation vanished and she was left to nurse the pulpy remains of her self-respect. Her actions suddenly seemed futile and pointless. She wished they could land quickly, pack up and go home. At least she would have the satisfaction then of finding herself in one piece. There didn't seem to be anything else worth looking forward to.

Peter let out a whistle as the balloon suddenly dropped. Unprepared, Emily shrieked. Untying two bags of ballast, Peter tipped out the sand and the balloon appeared to hang stationary again. The incident was over in a few minutes, but any confidence she had was shattered.

'It's only a pocket of air,' Peter said.

She looked at him, white with terror, unable to speak.

'You can't give in now.' He bent down and grasped her arms. 'Stand up. D'you hear me?'

Weak and trembling, she dug her fingers into the wickerwork.

'Look down . . . open your eyes.'

How could he be so cruel?

'Open them! That's right.'

He was supporting her, a hand under her armpit, his body hard at her back. Slowly her focus returned showing her a green carpet woven with patterns of hedges and winding lanes; here and there more elaborate with farms and wandering groups of cattle and sheep. London was a dark haze in the distance.

'It's such a long way down,' she whispered.

'D'you want me to make a landing?'

She would give her eyeteeth for that, but something made her hesitate. Swallowing hard, she asked: 'How far had yo planned to go?'

'Weather permitting – to the coast. I thought we'd have a picnic by the sea.'

'Let's do that,' she said in a very small voice; she had never seen the sea.

He was plainly astonished. 'You mean that?'

'I said so, didn't I?'

A long pause while cornfields and hopyards slid under their feet.

'I think . . .' he said slowly.

Another pause.

'What?'

'I think you've more courage than anyone I know.' He stroked her cheek.

She would fly over the sea if he wanted her to . . . provided she didn't die of fright before they got there. Buoyed up with the strength he'd given her, she leaned back on his shoulder revelling in this unique chance of being close to him. Above her head the wicker hoop guiding the ropes on their way to the balloon looked a wisp of a thing, no stronger than a dandelion clock, and the wicker floor seemed just as frail. But if it were all to collapse, she would still have had this moment. She toyed with the idea of telling him she loved him, but the struggle with words wasn't worth the risk of spoiling the moment.

Peter breathed deeply, stretching out his arm. 'Marvellous – the freedom up here. Every time I come on a flight I experience it. None of the stupid pettifogging rules of everyday life to push you about. All the pressures are swept away. I can be myself.'

She had never considered Peter to be anything but relaxed and perfectly confident before. This was a revelation.

'Don't you feel it?' he asked.

Slowly she nodded. With his support she could ride over insecurity. A strange bird-like independence coming to take its place.

'Look!' He was pointing to the horizon.

A strip of silver cut sky from land, pushing them farther apart all the time.

'The sea?' she asked, marvelling at this first sight. It looked so smooth and calm, spreading out to the edge of the world.

'The English Channel. Not long now.'

He moved away to check the altimeter and begin the routine for landing; stacking the remaining ballast inside the car, putting mooring ropes ready and securing all their belongings. She could see his mouth moving as he calculated height and wind strength. What would happen to them on the way down? Trees to catch them. Overshoot and they'd be in the sea. The hazards were endless. With absurd contrariness she wished they didn't have to land. Not because she was afraid, but because once they were back in the world, the unity that held them would begin to change.

The Channel had broadened into a living thing, a silver beach at its edge which moved back into rising sand dunes.

'That's Camber Sands,' Peter said. 'We'll make for there.' They had lost height, but apparently not enough. 'I'm going to release some of the gas.' He had the ripcord in his hand. 'When I tell you, jettison the remains of the ballast . . . not yet!' as she hauled up one of the bags. 'And be prepared for a bump. Whatever you do, hold tight. I don't want you hurt, you're too valuable.'

A rush of wind caught his words and she was left wondering if she had heard correctly. Looking round, she saw he was smiling. It was so easy to be deluded by people's expressions.

The hollow swish of escaping gas, and: 'Now!' he shouted. She pushed the heavy bag on to the lip of the car, watching sand shoot towards the puckered dunes. Another bag emptied and another, with a louder hissing of gas. The trail rope was already down, the grapnel dragging through sand and rushes, braking their speed. The ground came up to meet them with unexpected suddenness.

'Hang on!'

With a tremendous shock, the car hit the ground, throwing them together. Hamper, cushions and rugs broke loose and tumbled in a heap with spilled sandwiches and crockery. A capricious wind plucked up the collapsing silk envelope with a tug that dragged the groaning car over the sand, jolting the breath out of them.

'Damn!' Peter said with quiet venom, and then: 'I'm sorry . . . it's all . . . my fault,' as they bumped along.

Gradually the wind gave up the tussle, leaving the balloon writhing. They scrambled out and fought with its death throes, hampered by loose sand, straining to gather everything into the car. The work was surprisingly long and strenuous and by the time they had finished, Emily was worn out with combined excitement and effort.

'I'm about done,' she said, collapsing in the sand. She pushed a hand through her hair which had fallen over her shoulders. 'But at least I'm all in one piece and the breeze is a treat.'

Peter laughed and caught her hand, squatting in the sand beside her. 'Emily . . .'

'What?'

'You're so . . .' he hesitated, the laughter disappeared and an inner seriousness touched him. 'If it wasn't for the war . . .' he began and stopped again.

'War?'

'Oh, what's the point!' He stood up, releasing her hand. 'We haven't had our bubbly. After all that effort we deserve it.' He rummaged in the hamper and produced a bottle of champagne and a cup without a handle. 'We shall have to take turns, I'm afraid. Everything else is smashed.' He eased out the cork, but the champagne was thoroughly shaken and the cork shot out with a report like a pistol, followed by a jet of foam. He grabbed a cup, blowing sand out of it.

'Here's to us,' giving the cup to Emily.

'To us!'

They were laughing; taking turns to drink. From beyond the dunes she could hear seawater frothing on the shore, tantalizing with whispered promises of things unknown. She could smell its freshness and taste salt on her tongue. A great longing filled her.

'I feel sort of lightheaded,' she said. There was a strange sensation at the base of her skull and a feeling that she was still floating up there in the sky. Peter came to sit by her and as she turned to give him the cup, leaned close. Their noses bumped.

'And damn again,' he said. 'I don't seem to be very successful at kissing you.'

She expected him to try again, but he didn't and the easy companionship was replaced by a discouraging silence. Emily rubbed her nose, resenting the way things were turning out. The make-believe world in the balloon shrank to a speck.

'What do you mean about war?' she asked, just to get rid of the silence.

He was examining the cup he held as if it were a rare museum piece. 'Just that it's inevitable.'

'Nonsense!'

'It isn't nonsense, you know.' He looked at her openly. 'I don't suppose it will last long, but there are bound to be dangers.'

It was an odd conversation for a sunny day. War seemed remote, listening to seagulls and quiet wind in the rushes. She took a handful of sand and watched it trickle through her fingers. Like time, running away. Soon it would be time to go and nothing was resolved. All those inflated feelings were so much hot air. After all, what had she done? Dropped some paper into the streets of London! A very insignificant gesture.

'And it's because of those dangers I can't say more than I hope we'll always be friends. You are such a splendid girl, so full of courage – a chap couldn't ask for a better companion.' He was moved in a way she had never seen before; hesitating then going on with a burst of words: 'If only I could see into the future and be sure of coming through safely, I would . . .' He left the sentence unfinished, but it didn't matter because she understood exactly what he meant. There was enough joy and to spare, treasuring the offer of his friendship, never mind the rest. The future could take care of itself. A whole way of life stood between them, but instead of being divided, miraculously they were closer together. She gathered in her happiness, loving him all the more and when he said:

'We can be friends, can't we?' said spontaneously:

'For always . . . no matter what happens.'

He threw the cup in the sand, pulled her to her feet and hugged her until she thought her ribs would crack, then kissed her properly.

'Come on,' he said. 'We can't go back home and say we never saw the sea. After all we've both come a very long way.'

It was true. The distance stretched back and back, not in measurable miles, but in experience. So many failures lay behind – and a few successes. Ahead, a troubling future.

Taking Peter's hand she climbed with him between the rushes to the crest of the dune. The magnificence of the sea opened before her. She would never forget this first real view of it, a sapphire in the crown of a perfect day. They looked at each other; then, too full to stay still any longer, ran down into the white-gold of the deserted beach.

APPENDIX

4 August 1914
War between England and Germany was declared. Almost immediately Mrs Pankhurst called on the Suffragettes to cease their militant acts and channel their efforts into helping to defend their country.

11 January 1918
Through their valiant war efforts women proved beyond doubt that their position as active members of the nation could no longer be denied. The right to vote was given to those over thirty years of age.

14 June 1928
Emmeline Pankhurst died.

2 July 1928
Royal assent given to the Bill extending equal voting rights to men and women over twenty-one years of age.

ACKNOWLEDGEMENTS

I would like to thank the following people for their valuable help and encouragement.

Antonia Raeburn, for her personal advice and guidance, and for her outstanding book THE MILITANT SUFFRAGETTES (published by Michael Joseph Ltd).

Mrs H. M. Cooke, for her memories of her Suffragette cousin, the late Dora Benson.

Hilda Cole, for her careful research.

Marjorie Darke